SURREAL ABSURDITY

JIM LIVELY

TREATY OAK PUBLISHERS

PUBLISHER'S NOTE

This is a work of fiction. None of the characters or events is based on actual people, living or dead, or their lives or circumstances. Any similarities are a coincidence and purely unintentional.

**Printed and published in
the United States of America**

TREATY OAK PUBLISHERS

ISBN ⸱ 978-1-943658-69-5

also by Jim Lively

ABERRANT BEHAVIOR
PUNITIVE DAMAGES
THE PUZZLE AESTHETIC

Available on Amazon

DEDICATION

Dedicated to my three friends,
Gretchen Neary, Debbie Slaughter, and Joann Stokes.
I am grateful to each one of them for their friendship,
sense of humor, inspiration, and depth of personality.

CHAPTER 1

W*hat the hell?*
Charles's eyes popped open wider when he unfolded that day's *Dallas Morning News*. The lead article in the Metropolitan News section read:

NORTH DALLAS WOMAN ARRESTED ON SUSPICION OF MURDER

Jamie Simon was arrested this morning without incident in her North Dallas home and charged with first-degree murder in the death of Johnny Ross, an employee of The Adolphus Hotel.

Mrs. Simon was an employee of Ronda Graves, DVM, for several years at the Preston Tree Animal Clinic. As an employee, she had access to the lab at Ms. Graves's clinic, from which she allegedly stole several vials of ketamine. When administered in small doses, the drug is used to calm animals while they are undergoing certain medical procedures. Ketamine can be fatal to animals or humans if they ingest large doses of it.

According to police department spokesman Randel Scott, when Mrs. Simon was taken into custody for the theft of the ketamine, she surprised the arresting officers by confessing not only to the theft but also to the murder of Mr. Ross.

Charles tossed the newspaper aside and closed his eyes.

Oh my God. What if Jamie Simon told the police she was really trying to poison me? I thought this whole nightmare was over! He opened one eye. *Will I have to testify in court?*

Charles's cell phone buzzed on the coffee table. He picked it up. "Hello?"

"Is this Charles Pierce?"

"Yes."

"This is Detective Gonzales, Dallas Police Department."

"I would like to think you're calling me to just see how I'm doing. More likely, though, I assume you want to talk about Jamie Simon. I read the article in the newspaper."

"That's correct, Pierce. I have some questions I need to ask you—like why didn't you tell me about Jamie Simon being on your cruise last year?"

Charles swallowed. "Detective, did she tell you about our conversation on the last day of the cruise?"

"You mean how she had confessed to you that she had been trying to kill you?"

"Yes. I told her I was remorseful for the pain I had caused her in the trial last year, resulting in the denial of her husband's experimental treatment for cancer." Charles ran a hand over the top of his head. "I didn't want to pursue the matter any further."

"I assume you remember the conversation you and I had before you left for the cruise?"

Charles hesitated. "Y-y-es, Detective. You told me the ketamine poisoning case was closed."

"Do you recall me asking you if you'd thought of anything you'd forgotten to tell the police about the case?"

"Yes."

"Then why didn't you tell me about her confession to you?"

"Detective, to be honest, I hadn't forgotten to tell you about anything. Her confession happened on the cruise. I had no knowledge that she was the culprit when you and I talked before my trip." He sat up straight. "Listen, I just want this whole matter to be behind me. I thought she had suffered enough."

"Pierce, you're a lawyer, right?"

"You know I am."

"Well, as a lawyer, I assume you're aware that under Texas law, you can be charged with a Class A misdemeanor for failing to report an offense that resulted in serious bodily injury or death." His voice was tight as he enunciated each word.

"No, Detective. I haven't studied criminal law since my first year in law school." He stood up and faced the back windows. "Are you going to charge me with a crime?"

"You obviously had knowledge that a serious crime had been committed, but you didn't disclose that fact to me or, as far as I know, any other authority."

Charles sucked in a quick breath, and then his attorney skills kicked in and he decided not to say anything.

After waiting several seconds, Detective Gonzales said, "I haven't decided yet if I'm going to charge you with anything. My reason for calling is that I want you to cooperate fully with the police if this case should go to trial. I can't emphasize it enough when I say 'fully.'"

Charles rubbed his forehead. "I thought Jamie had already confessed to all the crimes involving ketamine." His tone turned to a whine "Why would you possibly need me to testify at a trial?"

"She has, Pierce. Nonetheless, you know how sometimes people change their stories. Their defense attorneys look for ways to invalidate the confession on some technical ground. I can't tell you how many times I've seen people confess, only to end up in court having a full-blown trial."

"I see. It sounds like you're implying that maybe someone in your department didn't follow proper procedure and botched the confession." His tone became calm, with a hint of guarded haughtiness.

"I'm not implying a damn thing," the detective snapped. "I just don't want to blow this case. That's why we may need you to be all-in on securing her conviction. I don't wanna have to charge you with a crime, Pierce, but I sure as hell will if you don't play ball."

"Play ball?" He smirked. "Detective, that sounds like a threat."

"You interpret it any way you wish."

Charles took a deep breath and exhaled loud enough so Gonzales could hear it. "Anything else, Detective?"

"You don't have any plans to leave the country anytime soon, do you?"

"No. I plan on being in Dallas for the foreseeable future."

"Okay, Pierce. I will be in touch."

"Yes, Detective."

Charles tossed his phone on the table.

God, I hope I don't have to testify in this case. What did he mean by "play ball?" He crossed his arms over his chest. *No way will I testify under oath to something other than the truth!*

CHAPTER 2

He was deep in his train of thought and shook himself out of it when his phone rang again. He picked it up and pressed the green button. "Hello?"

"Hi, Charles, this is Felicia."

"Felicia! It's been a long time," he gushed. "So nice to hear a friendly voice. How the hell are you doing?"

"I'm doing well. How about you?"

Charles grimaced. "Well, except for a phone call I received just now from a Dallas detective, I'm doing great."

"Did you say 'detective'? What was that all about?"

"Remember the ketamine poisoning cases at the Nasher Sculpture Center and The Adolphus Hotel? Well, the police finally nabbed the woman who was responsible for them."

"Yes, I remember the cases, but what do they have to do with you?"

"I didn't mention this to you before, but I was the intended target of the perpetrator, Jamie Simon. She was the plaintiff's wife in a case I defended. I represented the health insurance company when her husband sued it over a claim denial. The insurance company won the trial, her husband died, and the widow held me responsible." He paced in front of the windows. "She desperately wanted to exact her revenge by poisoning me with ketamine. The detectives investigating the case found that I was the one common denominator with all the poisonings."

"Really?"

"Yes, believe it or not, this woman took the same cruise as me. She even tried to poison me while we were at sea. The last day of the cruise, she confessed she was responsible for all the poisonings, including that young employee at The Adolphus Hotel. The detective wants me to testify to her confession if the matter goes to trial."

"Wow, Charles! That's incredible. I assure you my reason for calling is not that dramatic."

He laughed. "I'm relieved, Felicia. So why did you call me?"

"First of all, let me ask you a question. How's your transition from trial lawyer to visual artist progressing?"

"Nine months into it, I would have to say okay." He stopped pacing to stare out the window. "But as I've mentioned many times, art is a passion. There's no way I could've thought I'd make a sustainable living at it. However, I can report I'm doing better with sales than anticipated."

"I'm not surprised. When you set your mind on something, you're like a bullet train hurling down a track at a hundred miles an hour. Besides, I just checked out your website before I called. You're damn good, old friend."

Charles smiled. "The unfettered bias of a good pal. But thank you. I'm sure you didn't just call to praise my art, though, did you?

"No. As you suspect, I do have an ulterior motive. I know you're comfortably retired from practicing law. However, do you have any desire in perhaps doing some pro bono work? With your interest in art and your experience with fiduciary law, I thought you might be a perfect fit for this little endeavor. Care to at least hear about it?"

"Okay, I'm intrigued." He whirled around to face the kitchen. "Shoot."

Felicia paused to take a sip of what he presumed to be her morning coffee. "As you know, I'm one of the managing partners of my firm. It's one of my responsibilities to oversee the firm's commitment to provide a certain amount of pro bono work to the community. Are you familiar with CDADA, short for Contemporary Dallas Art Dealers Association?"

"Yes. I always attend CDADA's spring and fall art tours of the galleries. Beyond that, I really don't know what they do."

"As you may expect, CDADA is a 501(c) nonprofit. The owner of one of the participating galleries contacted John Sullivan in our firm. John's a huge art collector. The owner told John they had a problem with a prior managing director of CDADA, a woman named Cindy Stapler. Apparently, it was discovered that she had absconded with some of CDADA's funds."

"So the director got caught with her hand in the cookie jar, eh?"

Felicia laughed. "Well, that's another way of putting it, I guess."

"You want me to go review the matter and provide some guidance to CDADA's members?" He opened a drawer and took out a pencil.

"That's correct."

"Felicia, as you well know, besides the theft issue, there're some potential tax ramifications for using 501(c) funds for unauthorized purposes, whether it was done illegally or not."

"That's why you're perfect for the job. You may even be invited to exhibit your art at one of the galleries. A win-win, as I see it."

"Okay, I'll do it. Whom should I contact?"

"Sam Sterling. She's the owner of the Trinity River Gallery in the Dallas Design District and on the CDADA board of directors. I'll email you all the contact information."

"Sam's a female?"

"Short for Samantha." Her tone indicated an eye roll.

"I'll await your email. Oh, and let's meet for dinner sometime to catch up."

"Will do. Thanks again, Charles."

I wonder what I'm getting myself into here.

CHAPTER 3

Charles received Sam Sterling's email address from Felicia and right away sent her a message offering his services pro bono to assist CDADA. Sam invited him to the Trinity River Gallery to meet with her the following Monday since the gallery would be closed to the public.

At the agreed-upon time, Charles pulled his FIAT Spider up to the Trinity River Gallery, which was located on Levee Street at the edge of the Dallas Design District. He had visited the front part of the gallery before during one of CDADA's art tours. The back of the building was nestled in the green space that surrounded the levee of the Trinity River.

Only a few lights were on in the gallery. Charles made his way to the front door and attempted to turn the doorknob, but it was locked. He located the doorbell and pushed it.

After a few minutes, a woman cracked the door open and said, "Hello, may I help you?"

"Hello. I'm Charles Pierce," he said. "Are you Sam Sterling? I believe we have an appointment to meet today."

"Yes, Charles. Please come in. I'm a little careful opening the door to strangers. While our location has a certain bohemian charm, crime is pretty prevalent in the area."

"I understand completely."

Charles entered the gallery, and Sam locked the door behind them. She was a lovely, thin, pale woman in her late forties with dark hair and blue eyes.

"As per the instructions in your email," she said, "I've located all the documents I could find related to CDADA. I hope they'll provide you with everything you need to review the matter. Let's go into my conference room."

Charles followed her to the room. She motioned toward a chair. "Please have a seat at my conference table. All the papers are right there in the files."

He sat down, flipped open the first file, and paused. "Sam, this may take me a while to sift through all of these papers. If you have something you need to be doing, I'll be just fine here by myself."

"Thank you, Charles. I'll take you up on that. I'll be in the gallery adjusting the lights for an opening we're having Saturday evening. Let me know if you need anything."

"Will do."

Charles spent almost thirty minutes reviewing all the governing documents for CDADA. Once he had found and read the bylaws, he was finished. As he had anticipated, they contained very narrow requirements for how CDADA's funds could be used. Any variance from those requirements threatened the association's tax-exempt status. Charles organized the files and stacked them on the conference table. Then he exited the office in search of Sam. He found her perched at an unsafe angle on a ladder, focusing lights on a huge painting at the back of the gallery. To avoid startling Sam, he waited for her to notice his presence.

She looked down. "I'm sorry, Charles. I didn't know you were there."

"I didn't want to frighten you and cause you to fall off the ladder."

Sam laughed. "Well, I certainly appreciate that. I do tend to take risks at times. Are you all done with your review?"

"All done."

"What are the next steps, then?"

"I think it would be appropriate for me to meet with all the association's directors so we can discuss how to handle the matter involving the former managing director."

Sam climbed down from the ladder. "I'll send out an email tomorrow and try to arrange a meeting."

"Sounds good. By the way, do you own or lease the other side of the building as well?" He jerked a thumb over his shoulder.

"Yes, I lease the whole building. On the other side, I house all the paintings I have yet to hang or ship back to the artists." She collapsed the ladder and laid it on the floor against the wall. "There's a bunch of empty space. Would you care to see it?"

"Sure, if it's not too much trouble."

"This way."

Charles followed her over to a door that led to the other side of the building. It opened into a wide hallway that connected a series of rooms that must have been used for offices at one time.

"I use the back room as storage for my tools and packing materials," Sam said, pointing down the hallway. "This middle room is where I store all the artwork that's not currently on exhibit. The room at the front is pretty much empty except for some boxes."

"This is a nice space," Charles said. "It would make a perfect art studio."

"Do you know an artist who would like to sublease the space?"

Charles gave her a slight bow. "You're standing next to him."

"Really? You're an attorney and an artist?"

Charles fished a business card out of his wallet and handed it to Sam. "This is my website if you would like to check out my work."

She took the card. "I'll do that." She stared at his card for a moment, then tapped it against her fingertips. "Let me think about this whole art studio thing. Where's your studio now?"

"I don't have a dedicated studio. My paintings and supplies are strewn throughout my apartment. It's not an ideal arrangement."

"I can certainly understand that. I'll be in touch about the meeting and the studio rental."

* * *

A WEEK LATER, Charles received an email from Sam.

> Hi, Charles. Are you available next Monday
> to meet with all of CDADA's directors at 4:00
> p.m.? All the galleries are closed on Mondays.
> By the way, I checked out your website. I
> like your art. Quite creative. Let's discuss the
> leasing arrangements after the meeting on
> Monday. Of course, this assumes you still
> have an interest in the space.

Charles scratched his head. *Do I really want to
make this kind of commitment?*

CHAPTER 4

Charles arrived at the Trinity River Gallery at 4:00 p.m. on the dot. The small lot in front was full, so he located an empty parking space several blocks down the street. As he was exiting his FIAT Spider, someone coughed from the side of a dilapidated building. He locked his car and walked toward the gallery entrance. When he glanced in the direction of the sound of the coughing, a man in disheveled clothes sank to his knees, moaning and vomiting.

"Sir, are you okay?" Charles said.

The man did not bother to look around. "Get the hell out of here. You're trespassing on my property."

Charles thought, since he's walking on a public sidewalk, how could he be trespassing on anybody's property. *Best not to say anything and just keep walking.*

When he reached the front of the gallery, he peered through the window. A group of people sat around the table in Sam's conference room. He tried to open the front door, but it was locked. The same as his earlier experience, he rang the doorbell.

After a few minutes, Sam pulled the door open. "Right on time. We just wrapped up a brief meeting on a few agenda items."

Charles entered the gallery, and Sam relocked the door behind him.

"I met one of your neighbors down the street," he said. "The man didn't seem to care much for me."

She gave him a puzzled look. "What do you mean?"

"As I was walking up the street toward the gallery, I saw a man vomiting on the side of one of the buildings. When I asked if he was okay, he told me to get out of here because I was trespassing."

Sam smiled. "Probably a homeless guy. While we're technically located in the Design District, we're definitely in a fringe and developing area. I have to be very cognizant of my surroundings when I venture outside alone."

"Well, you did say you're located in a bohemian neighborhood."

"Yes, indeed. Come on, let me introduce you to the board."

She turned around and Charles followed Sam into her conference room.

"Hey, everyone, this is Charles Pierce," she said. "He's the attorney I mentioned to each of you. He has reviewed the issue we have with our past managing director."

He made his way around the room, shaking hands with each of the eight members, and then took the vacant seat at the end of the table as he surveyed the group. "Shall I begin?"

John Foxton, the owner of Foxton Heller Gallery,

spoke first. "Yes, please do. But let me first thank you on behalf of all of us for agreeing to do this for free."

Charles nodded. "You're very welcome. I hope my assistance will be of value to the association."

Charles spent several minutes discussing the part of the association's governing documents that related specifically to the matter at hand. He emphasized the adverse tax ramifications the association faced because its tax-exempt funds had been used for purposes the governing documents had not contemplated.

When he paused, John said, "Are you telling us we still have a tax problem, even though we had nothing to do with Cindy Stapler's pilfering of these funds?"

Charles grimaced. "Yes, I'm afraid that's definitely the case."

Chris Stephens, owner of Stephens Contemporary Gallery, said, "That doesn't seem fair. How could we've known she was going to use the association's money for her own purposes?"

Charles said, "That's irrelevant under the tax code."

"So what are our options?" Sam said.

"Well, there really is only one option," Charles said. "You need to get the funds back and thoroughly document in your minutes what happened and the actions taken by CDADA to recover the funds. Since you're a nonprofit organization, I doubt the IRS will be too harsh with penalties. By the way, how much money are we talking about here?"

"Almost ten grand," John said. "Charles, we have since learned why Cindy took the money. Her son has some mental problems. Long story short, he has even killed a man. Cindy's a single mom and only made about twenty thousand a year as our managing director. She also substitute teaches to try to make ends meet. She took the money to post bail for her son, after he was charged with murder. We all discussed this matter before you came today and pretty much decided to write off the loss. There's no way we would turn this matter over to the police. Besides being gallery owners, we're all artists and caring individuals. While what Cindy did was wrong, we forgive her. That being said, I don't want to lose our tax-exempt status."

"It's possible Cindy could get a loan from a third party," Charles said, "and repay the association. I recommend the funds be returned in full to CDADA in some manner. You don't want to jeopardize your tax-exempt status."

"Thank you," Sam said. "I think we have a lot to discuss here."

"Anyone have any further questions for Charles?" John said.

Everyone at the table shook their heads. Sam said, "Let's not take up any more of his time, then. Come on, Charles, I'll see you out."

"Thanks, Sam. Nice to meet you folks."

He exited the conference room and waited for Sam to follow. As they made their way to the gallery door, she said, "Thank you again for advising us on this issue."

"I'm sorry I couldn't deliver a better option on how to handle it."

"Well, at least we can now make an informed decision. By the way, I have a lease for the studio rental ready for you. Would you like me to email it?"

Charles smiled. "Sure, that would be great. I hope I can afford it."

"I think you'll be pleasantly surprised. In fact, it should be move-in ready in about three weeks."

"Wow, that's great news. I look forward to reading the lease."

Sam unlocked the door and held it open for him.

He said, "Good luck with everything."

"Thank you."

Charles walked down the old, decrepit sidewalk toward his Spider. Soon he arrived at the location where he had earlier seen the man vomiting. He glanced over to the side of the building, but no one was there. Shrugging, he assumed the man had moved on. As he got closer to his car, he noticed something under the windshield wiper. It was a crinkled and folded discolored white paper. Charles unfolded it. Its misspelled message warned: Prvate parking! No trespassing

What's this area's obsession with trespassing, anyway? I don't see any signs or markings to indicate private parking.

Charles slid the paper into his pocket and walked

around all sides of his car, examining the exterior. Satisfied no one had tampered with it, he unlocked the car and drove the short distance to his downtown apartment.

CHAPTER 5

Charles received an email from Sam the next morning containing the sublease agreement for the artist studio. Without reading the email, he opened the attachment containing the agreement and perused the sublease. The rent was a flat fee of $500 a month for the fifteen-foot-by-twenty-five-foot space. The rest of the terms and conditions were standard for that type of sublease.

My God, this is great! Sam did say I would be pleasantly surprised. She wasn't mistaken.

The email reminded Charles that the space would be available for him to occupy in about three weeks. He replied right away, agreeing to the terms and conditions of the sublease and thanking Sam for her generosity.

* * *

THREE WEEKS TO the day later, he received another email from Sam. It read:

> Hi, Charles. Your studio space is ready except for a little cleanup. Would you like to stop in late this afternoon and check it out? The gal-

lery closes at 5:00 p.m., but I will still be here
with my assistant, doing some paperwork.
Just ring the doorbell.

Charles indicated he would be at the gallery at
5:00 p.m.

* * *

AT 5:00 P.M., Charles pulled up to the gallery and
parked in one of the spaces right in front. As he
approached the door, he shot a glimpse in the direction where he had encountered the angry man a few
weeks earlier. He half expected the man to appear
from the side of a building to warn him again about
trespassing. Nothing was in the area but a few parked
cars and a feral cat poking its head in a discarded box
leaning against the gallery's exterior wall.

Charles pushed the doorbell. A young woman
in her late twenties opened the door a few inches.
In an Eastern European accent, she said, "Are you
Charles?"

"That's me."

The woman pulled the door open wider. "Please
come in. I'm Mary, Sam's intern."

Charles entered the gallery, and she locked the
door behind them. He said, "I'm pleased to meet you,
Mary. You have a beautiful accent. May I ask where
you're from?"

She smiled. "So you don't think I'm from Texas,

do you?"

"Not with that accent."

"Where do you think I'm from?"

He paused as if he could get it right, given a few more seconds. "My guess is Russia."

"Well, I do speak Russian, but I am from Estonia."

"Really? Are you a student studying abroad then?"

"Yes, I'm getting my master's in art history at SMU."

"Good for you. That's a good school. I got my law degree from there."

Sam appeared at the opening of the gallery that separated the front exhibition area from the rear area. "Hi, Charles, I was just checking on your space to make sure the workers had it ready. I see you've met Mary."

"Yes. We're getting acquainted."

Sam waved her arm toward the side door. "Care to go have a look at your space?"

"I can't wait." He turned to the younger woman. "So pleased to meet you, Mary. You'll be seeing a lot of me very soon."

She smiled. "Nice to meet you, Charles."

He followed Sam into the rear exhibition space and through the side door, which led to where Charles's space was located. She stopped when they reached the entrance to the studio and said, "Check this out." Sam slid a huge door that was on a track to the side. "I thought you might like a giant entrance to your gallery for large pieces of art, so I had my guys enlarge the door opening and construct this gliding slider door."

The rectangular studio consisted of museum-quality white walls, track lighting, and stained concrete floors.

His eyes swept the entire space. "Wow, this is very cool," he gushed. "Thanks."

"When do you think you might move in?"

"This weekend."

"That's good timing. We have an opening for our new exhibit next Saturday. If you're set up by then, you can open your studio during our event."

"That's great, Sam. I'll make sure I'm ready. By the way, does my studio have a name?"

She pondered the question a moment. "Since you have the only studio so far, how about we call it Studio 1?"

"Perfect. Do you mind if I get some vinyl letters to go above the door with the name?"

"Not at all, Charles. Stop by the office when you're done here and pick up the keys to the gallery and to your studio."

"Will do. Did you get my check for the first month's rent?"

Sam smiled. "Already deposited. Thanks for being so timely."

"My pleasure."

This will definitely be a new adventure.

CHAPTER 6

Charles hired a local moving company to transport to his new studio his easel, art table, midcentury modern couch, and two midcentury modern chairs he had been keeping in storage. Within a couple of hours, all the items were delivered, and he organized the studio to his liking.

As he sat down on the couch to admire his new space, his cell phone rang. "Hello?"

"Pierce, this is Detective Gonzales."

Charles grimaced. "How are you, Detective?"

"I've been better. The reason I'm calling is because the Jamie Simon case is going to trial after all."

Charles sighed, "Is her defense counsel challenging the legitimacy of the confession?"

"Yes, damn it!"

"Do they have any leg to stand on?" Charles said.

"When you and I spoke earlier, you asked if someone in the department had dropped the ball. Well, the answer is yes. You remember Detective White?"

"Yes, you both were investigating the ketamine poisoning cases."

"He retired from the force, and they assigned me a young guy named Grayson to train as my new partner. He seems like a smart enough guy but is still green as hell behind the ears. When we brought Jamie in for questioning, I thought this was going to be a slam dunk. I briefly left Grayson and her in the room together so I could get the file on the case. To my horror, Grayson questioned her alone. He forgot to give her the Miranda warning. As a lawyer, you know what that means."

Charles groaned. "So she must have confessed to killing The Adolphus Hotel employee and the attempted killing of me before she was read her rights. Which means all of it is inadmissible at trial."

"Precisely. Pierce, I need this conviction, or otherwise, I'm toast."

"What do you mean, you're toast?"

"As a detective training a new guy, I committed the cardinal sin of leaving him alone with a suspect. I'm due for a pay raise. With this stain on my record, the department may even demote me."

"But Detective, the confession is only one component. Don't you have her theft of the ketamine from the veterinarian to tie her to the crimes?"

The other man sighed. "Yes, but it turns out that Jamie and the veterinarian are old sorority sisters. Let's just say she'll be a hostile witness. That's why I need you to testify in court about her confession to you on the cruise."

"What makes you think I won't be a hostile witness?"

The detective raised his voice. "Because I will arrest you on a charge of failure to report Jamie's confession to the police. I don't think even retired lawyers would want a Class A misdemeanor on their record. Am I correct, Pierce?"

Charles paused. "A little *quid pro quo*, eh, Detective?"

"Call it whatever you like, but you need to cooperate with the prosecutor's office. Jamie Simon has committed several heinous crimes, and I don't want her to walk because of a technicality."

"Okay, I'll testify about the confession."

"I'll be in touch."

"Goodbye, Detective."

Charles hung up before Detective Gonzales could say anything further.

Not much I can do about this matter except make sure I'm not asked to do anything unethical.

No longer in the mood to do anything creative, Charles decided to lock his studio and head back to his apartment. As he drove home, he kept thinking about having to testify in the trial. He dreaded the inevitable.

CHAPTER 7

The following Saturday evening, Charles arrived at the Trinity River Gallery thirty minutes before the scheduled opening. He wanted to have time to get organized and prepared, should any visitors attending the reception make their way back to Studio 1.

He straightened some of his paintings of new works he had hung on his wall yesterday, made sure his card holder on the shelf near the door was full of business cards, and opened a nice bottle of Cabernet Sauvignon to let it breathe. He opened his small refrigerator to check on his supply of Chardonnay. Five bottles of Rombauer were chilled to perfection.

Content with how Studio 1 looked, Charles opened a bottle of Chardonnay and poured a generous glass for himself. He stared down, smiled at his wine glass, and thought, *I may be an attorney-turned-artist, but I have a little marketing in me as well.*

He had designed custom glassware with a 'Studio 1' insignia imprinted on the side. His rush order had arrived the Friday before Saturday's opening.

He turned on some Brian Eno mix on his stereo, sat in one of his studio chairs, and closed his eyes to enjoy the sensation of music and the effect of the glass of wine.

A stylishly dressed young couple appeared at the entrance of Studio 1. The man said, "Excuse me. Is your studio open?"

Charles sprung to his feet. "Sure, please come on in." Only the man had a half-empty glass of white wine in his hand, so he said, "Would you care for some more wine? If you like Chardonnay, I've just opened a nice Rombauer."

"I would love a glass of Rombauer," the woman said.

Charles poured her one. Then he gestured toward the man. "You can set that glass down if you prefer. I feel certain this wine is superior to whatever they're serving in the main gallery."

The man smiled. "You got a deal."

* * *

CHARLES MAINTAINED A steady flow of visitors to his studio spilling over from the gallery. While some were there strictly out of curiosity, most were young, trendy people with disposable income. The kind of people every gallery owner desires within its confines.

After a couple of hours, the number of visitors to Studio 1 dwindled to just a few infrequent guests. Charles checked his watch. The opening would be over in thirty minutes. He decided to see what was going on in the gallery.

As he approached the door of his studio, a thirty-something-year-old, heavy-set man stepped around the corner and blocked his path. The man entered Studio 1 and pulled the heavy, sliding door behind him with such force that it slammed closed and bounced back slightly open. Cigarette smoke and what was probably some cheap whiskey emanated from the man's breath. Dressed in blue jeans and a faded plaid work shirt, he had a crew cut and an unkempt beard.

Stepping back a few paces, Charles said, "Can I help you?"

The man's eyes darted around the room before staring at Charles. "You Pierce?"

Charles hesitated. "I'm Charles Pierce. May I ask who you are?"

The man took a step forward and snarled in low voice, "So you're the bastard who caused my family a load of trouble."

The wheels turned in Charles's brain. *The bastard who caused my family a load of trouble. What the hell does that mean?*

Charles laid his palm on his sternum, "I... I t-t-think you m-m-must have me mistaken for someone else."

"I ain't mistaken."

Before Charles could reply, Sam peered in through the crack in the doorway. "Please come in, Sam," he called out.

Both men stared at the door as it slid farther

open. Sam entered Studio 1 and said, "I apologize if I'm interrupting."

Charles sighed. "No, I assure you that you're not interrupting anything. This gentleman and I were discussing some business, but we're finished now."

The man growled, "Later, Pierce." He turned and stomped toward the opening of Studio 1. The man glanced at the shelf that displayed Charles's business cards, several art magazines, and the gallery's brochures for upcoming exhibitions. He grabbed a handful of items and exited. Moments later came the sound of a disturbance in the hallway as magazines were ripped and tossed on the floor.

Charles and Sam both hurried to the door to peer out. Bits of magazines and business cards were strewn across the floor. The man was out of sight.

"God, I hope he doesn't cause more damage on his way out," Sam said.

"Sorry about that, Sam!"

"Charles, you look a little pale." She clutched Charles's arm. "What was that all about?"

"I have no earthly idea." Charles shook his head. "This strange guy just walks into my studio, slides the door shut, and accuses me of getting his family into trouble!"

Sam smiled. "Well, I guess it's a good thing I showed up, then."

"There's no telling what would've happened," he said as he rubbed his forehead "if you hadn't come in when you did."

"Have you ever seen him before?"

"No. How about you? Ever seen him in the gallery?"

"Not that I recall." Sam tilted her head a bit sideways, then straightened it. "I'm sure I'd remember him. But don't worry too much about it, though. You know, bohemian neighborhood and all. That's also why I keep a loaded pistol locked in my desk."

Charles's eyebrows shot up. "You own a gun?"

"I certainly do. Simone, my partner, and I took lessons and often go to the gun range for practice. I'm a pretty good shot. But she's actually a superior shot."

"Really? I haven't met Simone."

"You will someday." She winked at him.

"By the way, why did you come back here to Studio 1? Has the opening ended?"

"To your first question, I hear you're serving some pretty serious wine in here. I thought we might share a celebratory glass. As to the second question, the opening ended ten minutes ago."

"Celebratory glass?"

"Yes. We had a good night! One couple bought two paintings, and another guy showed some interest in a piece. I thought you'd like to celebrate your first opening in Studio 1."

Charles laughed. "Well, except for how it ended, I would agree with you. But hey, let's have a glass of wine. Do you care for Chardonnay or—"

"Definitely red, assuming it's not a Merlot."

"No. I have a nice Cab I think you'll enjoy."

Charles poured Sam a glass of Cabernet Sauvignon and himself a Chardonnay, then said, "I have to be honest, I'm still a little shaken about that strange guy. I can't fathom what he meant about me getting his family into trouble."

"Sorry, Charles," Sam said. "At least it wasn't a boring night. Did you have a good crowd come back here?"

"Yes. I had a steady flow all evening. Did you tell folks to wander back here, or did they just make it to my studio on their own?"

"Mary and I both encouraged patrons to pay a visit to our resident artist."

"Resident artist? I like that. Thank you."

"You're quite welcome." Sam checked her cell phone. "Well, time to shut it down for the evening."

"I'm going to clear some of these empty wine glasses from my studio, then I'm out of here as well."

* * *

CHARLES AND SAM left the gallery together. He said, "Are you parked close?"

"Yes, that's my car here." She pointed to a Mini Cooper about ten feet away. "One of the perks of being the gallery owner. I'm always first to arrive and always have a close parking place. What about you? Do you need a lift to your car?"

"No, thanks. I'm just half a block down."

"Okay, good night, Charles."

"Good night."

The night was cool and cloudy as Charles walked down the sidewalk in the direction of his FIAT Spider. From his peripheral vision, he spotted a dark figure run and disappear between two buildings. He froze in his tracks and stared in the direction of where he had last seen the figure. Charles shivered at the prospect of danger lurking in the shadows.

Is it that the guy who came to my studio? I better get to my damn car in a hurry!

His pace changed from walking to jogging toward his car, about fifty feet down the sidewalk in front of him. Charles fumbled in his pocket for his keys and hit the Unlock button on the remote. Once he reached his car and climbed in the front seat, he locked the door and started the engine. No one was in sight.

What's with this area? It always seems so sinister!

CHAPTER 8

After several weeks, Charles settled into a routine of painting every afternoon in his studio and celebrating the end of each day with a glass of Chardonnay. As was his custom, he would exit his studio and venture into the main part of the gallery to study the art on exhibit. It was a good way to decompress and get inspiration from other artists' creativity. If Sam or Mary were in the gallery, he would offer them a glass of wine.

In no time, Sam picked up on Charles's habit. If she were not on the phone, she would call out, "It's been a long day. I could sure use a glass of wine in here." He never answered except to appear a few minutes later with a glass in his hand. The artist-in-residence experiment was working out well for both of them. They discovered they had a lot in common. Both of them loved fine dining, wine, and contemporary art.

One evening as Charles was locking his studio, Sam rounded the corner of the hallway. "Any plans for dinner tonight?" she said.

He smiled. "No, unless you call popping a frozen dinner into a microwave 'plans for dinner.'"

"Care to try Oak down the street?" Sam jerked

her thumb over her shoulder. "It just opened a couple of months ago."

"Sounds good. I noticed it last week when I was driving back to my apartment one night."

"We could walk since it's only about four or five blocks."

"I don't know about that, Sam. I haven't had great experiences walking in this neighborhood just to my car. Why don't I drive? I'll bring you back here to pick up your car."

Over the course of dinner, they shared a bottle of Ridge East Bench Zinfandel. Sam said, "Are you enjoying living uptown?"

"It's pretty cool. Noisy at times. But that's part of living in a vibrant area. I just wish I owned my own place instead of leasing."

"I understand. I wish I owned the gallery."

"Where do you live, if you don't mind me asking?" Charles said.

"Simone and I live in old East Dallas. We have a cozy, 1930s bungalow."

"I would like to meet her sometime."

"My partner's a very private person. She doesn't care for crowds and openings at the gallery. You'll eventually meet her though."

"I look forward to it."

"How about you, Charles? I take it you're not married."

"That's correct. My wife died a few years ago. Now I'm a cranky, old bachelor." He shrugged. "So cranky, in fact, that I'm not even in any type of relationship."

Sam laughed. "I disagree. I've been around you enough to know you're not cranky. At times, you can even be quite charming."

"I seriously doubt that." He smiled. "But I'll take any compliment these days."

She gave his hand a gentle pat. "You're too hard on yourself. Besides, you're a talented artist."

"Thanks, Sam. I very much appreciate your kind words—so much so that I'm going to get the check."

As if on cue, the waiter delivered the check, and Charles grabbed it.

"Thank you."

"You're most welcome."

After dinner, Charles pulled his car up next to Sam's car in front of the gallery. Before exiting, she leaned over and gave him a quick but soft kiss on the lips. "Thank you for a lovely evening."

"Thank you, Sam."

Didn't she say 'partner' earlier?

CHAPTER 9

The next afternoon, Charles opened the front door of the Trinity River Gallery. He was eager to get started on a new series of paintings. The door to the gallery buzzed as it always did, alerting either Sam or Mary that someone had entered.

Mary appeared at the office door. "Hello, Charles."

"Hi, Mary. How are you doing this afternoon?"

"Fine, thank you. By the way, you had a visitor this morning."

"A visitor?"

"Yes, a man."

"Did he leave a name or a reason for why he was here to see me?"

"No, I told him you usually come in about this time every afternoon. He said he would be back then."

"What did he look like?"

She put her finger up to her chin as if that might help her remember the man's appearance. "I don't know. He was older, a little heavy set, . . . maybe in his fifties."

Charles surmised that everyone looked older to Mary since she was in her mid-twenties at best. "Do you recall what he was wearing?"

She shook her head. "Not really. Sorry."

"Well, was he dressed casually or dressed up?"

"I remember now. He was wearing a dark suit."

Charles smiled. "Okay, Mary. Sorry for the third degree. I guess it's just my attorney instincts kicking in."

"No problem." Mary reentered the office.

Charles made his way through the gallery back to his studio. He spent the next thirty minutes at tedious labor, stretching a new, thirty-inch-by-forty-inch canvas. Once finished, he took care as he secured it on his huge easel. Charles selected some neutral background colors and squeezed them onto his palette, along with some acrylic medium. He mixed the paints with the medium for several seconds.

Satisfied he had the correct color mix and texture, he applied the paint with a large brush he had purchased a few days earlier from The Home Depot for less than five dollars. Experience had taught him that he didn't need to waste money on fine art brushes for the first application of background paint.

After completing one coat, Charles leaned back in his chair and studied the canvas. He was reaching over to his palette to load his brush with more paint when someone knocked three times, hard and loud, on his studio door.

I wonder if this is my visitor from earlier today.

Charles rested his brush on the palette and walked the fifteen feet to his door. He slid it open an inch at a time, concerned by who might be waiting on the other side.

"Hello, Pierce," said Detective Gonzales.

Charles' eyes widened. "Detective. How did you know I had a studio here?"

"I'll get to that in a minute."

As he opened the door wider with a flourish, Charles said, "Please come on in and have a seat."

Detective Gonzales sat down in one of the mid-century modern side chairs. He grimaced. "These old chairs sure weren't made for comfort, were they?"

"No, but they're very stylish." Charles crossed his legs at the ankles. "At least that's what I told myself when I purchased them from a secondhand shop on Industrial Boulevard."

"I'm sure you know more about such things than I do."

"So, Detective, I assume you're here concerning the Jamie Simon case." Charles sat up straight. "Is it time for me to meet with the prosecutor to prepare for my testimony at trial?"

"That will happen soon. However, I'm here for another reason."

"Really!' He relaxed his posture just a bit. "What could that possibly be?"

Detective Gonzales fished a sealed, plastic bag out of his suit coat pocket. It bore a label marked *File 33, Evidence exhibit 17.* He held it up so Charles could examine its contents. "Ever seen this before?"

Charles gasped. Inside was one of his business cards. It had smudges and a slight tear, but his name, address, email, website, and phone number were still clearly legible.

"Where the hell did you find my card?"

The detective slipped the plastic bag back into his pocket and leaned forward in his chair toward Charles. "I was hoping you may be able to provide me with that answer."

Charles sighed. "Detective, I don't have the foggiest idea where the police discovered one of my cards!"

Detective Gonzales frowned. "I suspected you were going to say that, Pierce. Actually, it was found just a few blocks from here."

"But why is it being kept as evidence?"

"Because it was found at the scene of a crime."

Charles shook his head in disbelief. "What kind of crime?"

"Nothing serious. Just a run-of-the-mill burglary and theft."

"Burglary and theft?" Charles sank backward until he slumped in the chair.

"Yelp. The Home Depot on Lemmon Avenue."

"I was in there the other day buying some paint brushes."

"Could the card have fallen out of your pocket then?"

Charles shrugged. "I wasn't carrying any cards at the time."

"It could've been the burglar who left it there."

"Why would a burglar leave my business card at the scene of a crime? That doesn't make any sense."

Detective Gonzales shifted his weight in the chair.

"We don't know that the burglar left the card there. It might just have been a coincidence. Maybe your card fell out of the purse of some little old lady who visited your studio earlier."

"Where exactly at The Home Depot did you find the card?"

"The perpetrator jimmied the lock on one of the back doors to let himself him in. The card was on the floor just inside the door, along with some items from the store racks he had dropped or decided he didn't want to take."

"Was anything missing from the store?"

"The Home Depot is a huge store. The manager's still inventorying to determine what, if any, other items were stolen. He's pretty certain the guy made off with a couple of pipe wrenches."

"How would he know for sure pipe wrenches were taken?"

"They were part of a set on display near where the break-in occurred. The perpetrator used one of the wrenches to break a glass case full of expensive knives. That set off an alarm and probably caused him to make a quick exit."

Charles paused. "So this guy was scared out of his wits and wanted to get the hell out of the store. Yet he takes the time to place my card just inside the door. That doesn't even seem logical. Detective, it sounds like my card was deliberately planted there so the police would find it."

"Perhaps, Pierce. On the other hand, maybe that's

what the perpetrator wanted us to think."

Charles shot up in his chair. "What do you mean?"

"Never mind. Tell me, how long have you had your studio here?"

"Several weeks now."

Detective Gonzales jerked his head in the direction of the door to the studio. "I noticed when I came in here that you keep your business cards in a holder next to the door."

Nodding, Charles glanced at the heavy door Sam had installed, wishing it were bigger.

"Are they on display anywhere else?"

"A few are on the table just inside the gallery front door. Also, the gallery owner keeps some in her office in case she receives an inquiry about my art. The only other ones on display are in here." He pointed toward the shelf near the doorway.

"I see. Do you get a lot of visitors to your studio?"

"Not really, except during an exhibit opening. Then probably thirty to forty people come in here through the course of the evening."

"How many openings have there been since you've been here?"

Charles held up his index finger. "Just one so far."

"Do you keep your studio locked when you're not here?"

"Yes. But Sam, the gallery owner, and Mary, her intern, have keys and access."

Detective Gonzales rubbed his nose. "Are you always aware during the course of the evening when someone helps himself to one of your cards?"

"I'm busy socializing and trying to sell art, Detective. I'm not paying attention to whether someone takes a card or not."

The detective stood up. "Okay, Pierce. That's all I need for now."

Charles stood as well. "What about the Jamie Simon case? I assume you still want me to testify?"

"Most definitely. I haven't been notified yet when the prosecutor wants to schedule a meeting with you. Have a good day." He walked toward the door.

"You too, Detective. Oh, by the way, you know where to come, should you ever need any art for your office."

Detective Gonzales didn't stop or even turn around. But as he exited the studio, he waved his hand in the air in a manner some might interpret as dismissive.

Charles smirked. *Damn, I can't seem to avoid being involved with criminals!*

CHAPTER 10

It was 6:30 p.m. on Saturday. The Trinity River Gallery had scheduled an artist reception and opening for 7:00 p.m. Charles was preparing Studio 1 in anticipation of having visitors later in the evening. He followed the same routine as before. Paintings were straightened, wine glasses were set out, paints on his worktable were neatened, and ambient electronic music was cranked up on his stereo.

Satisfied with Studio 1's appearance, Charles poured himself a glass of wine and sat on his couch to take in the ambiance. His experience as the gallery's resident artist made him smile. He enjoyed painting in Studio 1 and during his tenure had been able to sell a couple of paintings along the way.

Sam had told him that tonight's guests would be the young, edgy, and beautiful crowd. Judging by the artist's paintings hanging in the gallery, Charles was certain of the edgy aspect. The artist specialized in large works incorporating various mediums, including blood and coffee.

At the sound of the buzzer of the front door to gallery, Charles rose to his feet. He poured himself another glass of wine and waited for those he hoped would be art collectors with disposable income.

Two young ladies in their early twenties were the first to venture into Studio 1. Neither had the obligatory glass of wine served in the gallery in their hands. Charles sized them up, trying to determine if they were old enough to drink. He decided to throw caution to the wind.

"Hi, I'm Charles. May I offer either one of you a glass of wine?"

They looked at each other as if to gain reassurance. One woman with long brown hair accented with a pink streak said, "Sure. Do you have Pinot Grigio?"

"No," Charles said, "but I have an exquisite Rombauer Chardonnay you may like."

She smiled. "Sure. How about you, Kristen?"

Kristen was tall and statuesque with dirty-blonde hair. "Why not?"

Charles poured two generous servings of Chardonnay into his custom-designed wine glasses and handed one to each woman. Both of them said, "Thank you."

The woman with brown hair extended her hand. "I'm Denise."

He shook her hand. "Pleased to meet you, Denise."

"Are you the artist?" Kristen studied his face.

"Yes, I'm the resident artist but not the artist exhibited in the gallery."

For the first time since entering Studio 1, they strolled across the room to look at Charles's paintings hanging on the walls. "This painting is awesome!" Denise gushed.

"Thank you. It's my latest." Charles walked up behind her. "I'm beginning a new abstract series incorporating a lot of texture and geometric shapes."

Kristen's phone chimed. "Do you mind if I sit down a minute and respond to this text?"

"Not at all. Make yourself at home."

Kristen sat in the chair near the opposite wall, facing Charles. She rested her wine glass on the side table next to her chair. Denise strolled throughout Studio 1, studying each piece of art. Charles wasn't certain if she were in fact interested in his art or was biding her time so she could get another glass of Chardonnay before exiting.

He glanced over at Kristen, who sat feverishly typing with her thumbs on her iPhone. She uncrossed her legs and parted them slightly. She was not wearing any underwear. Kristen looked up from her phone and made eye contact with him. She smiled, recrossed her legs, and continued typing on the screen.

I wonder if that little going-commando gesture was accidental or for my benefit?

Kristen stood up. "Denise, let's go check and see who's here."

Denise handed her empty wine glass to Charles. "Thank you, sweetie, for the wine."

"Of course. You're very welcome."

As they exited, a whole group of young people appeared at the entrance to Studio 1. A twentysomething, pale brunette wearing black yoga pants and a matching top said, "Wow, what a cool space."

"Are you the artist?" one of the young men said.

"I am. Please come in. Help yourself to some wine if you care for any."

The group drained the bottle of Chardonnay and part of the Zinfandel before they left. Group after group streamed into Studio 1. Charles could not speak to everyone, so he retired to his work chair. He made himself available if anyone had a question or a comment. At the first opportunity, he opened his refrigerator and pulled out another bottle of Chardonnay.

As he was uncorking it, a woman appeared at the entrance. "Is it okay to come in?"

"Of course. If you would like some Chardonnay, I've just opened this Rombauer. If you prefer red, the Zin on the table is quite excellent."

She smiled at Charles. "A glass of Chardonnay would be very nice."

He poured her one, handed it to her, and set the bottle on his coffee table. Something about her, different than the crowd of people who had preceded her, caught his eye. She was in her forties, slim, and attractive but in a rough, boyish sense. Her clothing consisted of a white T-shirt and faded-blue jeans. She did not appear to be wearing any makeup or jewelry. A tattoo on her left arm extended below her sleeve.

As he was about to tell her to make herself at home, his cell phone rang. "Excuse me while I get this." He walked over to his couch and sat down. "Hello?"

A man on the other end of the line said, "Is this Pierce?"

"Yes."

"Are you in your studio tonight?"

"I am. May I ask who's calling?"

Click. The man ended the call.

That's very strange. Why would someone ask if I was in my studio and then just hang up?

The woman made the rounds looking at all the paintings on exhibit in his studio. "Do you mind if I sit down for a few minutes?"

Her wine glass was empty. "Not at all," he said. "Would you care for another glass?"

Rather than sit in one of the two chairs, the woman eased herself onto the couch next to him. "I thought if I sat beside you, then you wouldn't have to reach so far to hand me the glass."

Suppressing a gasp, Charles poured them both one. He was now feeling the effects of the wine. With all the activity in Studio 1 throughout the evening, he could not remember how many glasses he had already drunk.

The woman extended her glass in his direction. "Cheers, Charles."

They clinked wine glasses. He said, "Salut."

"By the way, my name is Lynn."

"Nice to meet you, Lynn"

"Likewise."

As the closing of the gallery opening approached, Charles and Lynn still sat on the couch drinking wine.

A few more people straggled into Studio 1. From time to time, Charles would tell them to let him know if they had any questions.

"Do you think anyone else is coming in this evening?" Lynn said.

He checked the time on his phone. "Only a few minutes to go before the opening is over. I seriously doubt if anyone is going to make the trek back here."

"Well, let's make sure, then." She stood up, walked over, and slid the studio door shut. Then she rejoined Charles on the couch. She squeezed in close next to him and placed her left hand on his thigh. Lynn smiled and then gave him a kiss on the lips. She then stood up, straddled him, and whispered, "You don't mind, do you?"

Before Charles could respond, she kissed him, first on his cheek, then his mouth. He was both aroused and uneasy.

Something isn't right here. I've known this women for fifteen minutes.

"E-e-excuse me, L-l-lynn." He lifted her up and off his lap.

Eyes wide, she snapped, "What's wrong?"

"Nothing, really. I just think we better join the others in the gallery before they close."

They exited Studio 1 and Charles paused to lock the door. Lynn's cell phone buzzed. She stared at the screen for a few seconds and hurried away. She was about ten yards in front of Charles when they reached the main gallery area. Sam and Mary were standing at the bar the gallery used to serve wine during events. Lynn all but sprinted past them.

Charles shouted, "Are you okay, Lynn?"

She did not respond. The front door buzzed as she exited the Trinity River Gallery.

Charles jogged to the gallery door and cracked it open. He watched Lynn hail a waiting car half a block down the street. When she opened the door to climb into the passenger seat, the interior of the car was illuminated. Charles got a few seconds' glimpse of a man's face in the driver's seat before the car sped away down Levee Street.

Where have I seen him before?

Charles jerked himself up to his full height. That was the man who had accused him of somehow harming his family.

Charles locked the front door and joined Sam and Mary in the back gallery.

"Charles," Mary said, "you look like you've seen a ghost."

"I wish I had instead of what I actually saw."

"What was that all about?" Sam said.

"I'm not sure." He frowned and glanced toward the entrance. "I'm still trying to wrap my brain around it."

"Mary and I went back to your studio earlier to celebrate with a glass of your wine, and your door was closed. We thought maybe you had already left for the evening and we just missed seeing you leave."

Charles grimaced. "That woman shut the door."

"Why would she do that?" Mary said.

"Believe it or not, so we wouldn't be disturbed."

Sam laughed. "Do you want us to mind our own business?"

"Absolutely not." Charles waved his palms at them. "I want to tell you everything so maybe you can help me think this thing through. This woman came back to my studio toward the end of the evening. She had a different look than most of the other visitors. I can't quite put my finger on it. She was attractive and all, but not trying to be stylish, if that makes sense. Her name was Lynn, or at least that was the name she told me. Have either of you seen her before?"

"Not me," Sam said. "I can't say I had a good look at her, though."

Mary shook her head.

Charles continued. "This Lynn person joined me on the couch. We made conversation and had several glasses of wine. Quite out of the blue, she gave me a kiss. Then, she got up, slid the studio door shut, came back over, and climbed on my lap. That's when I sensed something wasn't kosher."

"But why would she do that," Sam said, "if there was something else nefarious going on?"

"I don't know. When I suggested we go to the main gallery, she became agitated. She was staring down at her phone and just walked away as I was locking my studio. Then you saw her storm right past you and out of the gallery." Charles bit his lip. "But this is the part where it gets downright *spooky*. I watched her get into a car with a man. His face was visible for a moment in the car's interior light when she opened the passenger door. I recognized the guy."

"Who was he?" Sam said.

"Do you remember the guy who threatened me during the opening shortly after I moved into my studio?"

She nodded. "The buzzed-cut, scruffy guy."

"That's him."

"Remind me, what did the guy say when he threatened you?"

Charles waved his arms. "He said something to the effect about me getting his family into trouble."

"Could it be related to one of your cases," Mary said, "when you practiced law?"

"I don't think so. It's not like I was a criminal prosecutor or anything. I was an insurance defense attorney. Although I did have one woman who tried to poison me when the insurance company I represented denied her husband's claim." Charles snorted. "But never did I have a case where I got someone into trouble."

"You'll have to tell us about that case sometime," Sam said.

"I will. In fact, I'm going to have to testify against her at trial very soon."

Mary said, "Wow!"

"I'm still perplexed as to why that woman came on to me," Charles said. "What was her motive?"

"Well, maybe she was trying to seduce you," Sam said.

"Do you think that she wanted to lure me outside to where that guy was waiting somewhere in the shadows?"

Sam said, "But why then would she just leave without saying a word?"

"She checked her phone as I was locking my studio. Maybe the guy texted her to call the whole charade off."

"Very strange," Mary said, adding a tsk-tsk.

"Definitely strange," Charles said. "Well, I've had enough excitement for one night. I think I'll head on home."

"Let's all leave together," Sam said. "You never can tell—our scruffy friend may still be lurking nearby."

All three of them were parked side by side in front of the gallery. Charles waited for Sam and Mary to pull away before he left the parking lot. During the short drive to his apartment, he never stepped on the brake and checked his rearview mirror every few seconds.

CHAPTER 11

On Monday morning, Charles's cell phone buzzed on the side table next to him. He took another sip of his coffee before he answered. "Hello?"

"Hello, Pierce. This is Detective Gonzales."

"Yes, Detective."

"I wanted to check your availability this Wednesday at 2:00 p.m. The prosecutor assigned to the Jamie Simon case wants to prep you for trial."

Charles shifted his phone in his hand so he could check his calendar. "Sure, that's not a problem. How much time will he need?"

"The prosecutor is a woman named Deborah Brannon, and she didn't say how long it would take. I would block off all afternoon to be on the safe side."

Charles snickered. "I don't have a busy schedule. That's not a concern."

"Okay. Her office is in the administrative building next to the criminal courthouse. I assume you're familiar with where that's located."

"Yes, Detective." Charles rolled his eyes.

"Her office is on the fifth floor. When you enter the building, take the bank of elevators on your immediate right to the fifth floor. Tell the person manning the reception desk that you have an appointment with Deborah."

"I can handle that."

They hung up and Charles stared out the window at downtown Dallas, his mind a blank.

* * *

AT 1:50 P.M. ON Wednesday, Charles exited the elevator onto the fifth floor of the administrative building where most of the Dallas County prosecutors had their offices. He approached the reception desk and waited for the young woman sitting there to acknowledge his presence.

The receptionist glanced up from her computer screen. "May I help you?"

Charles suspected she grew weary of having to ask the same question multiple times a day. "I have an appointment with Ms. Brannon. She should be expecting me."

The receptionist made a quick call. He stood in front of her, listening to one end of the conversation. She hung up and, without making eye contact, handed Charles a visitor's badge. "Room D-33, down that hall on your left."

Charles considered saying thank you but decided it would fall on deaf ears. He clipped the badge onto his sport coat pocket and made his way down the dingy gray hall as directed. As soon as he arrived at room D-33, he knocked three times on the closed door. From inside, a woman's voice called, "Come in.

It's open."

Charles opened the door and walked inside. Room D-33 was a small conference room containing a narrow, laminated table surrounded by laminated chairs. Seated at the head of the table was a thin, brunette woman. After Charles had waited motionless for a few seconds, she stood and said, "I'm Deborah Brannon. Please have a seat there, Mr. Pierce."

Charles settled into the chair she indicated. Deborah moved from the end of the table to sit across from him. Although she was attractive, she also wore a copious amount of dark eye makeup. It made her look a bit menacing.

"I'm sure Detective Gonzales informed you," she said, "that I'll be prosecuting the Jamie Simon case."

"Yes."

"I understand you're an attorney. What was your area of practice?"

From his own trial experience, Charles figured she already knew most, if not all, of the answers to the questions she was going to ask him. That was part of her due diligence in preparing for trial to avoid any surprises.

"Insurance litigation. I defended health insurers from suits filed by their insureds for claims denied."

"And that's how you first crossed paths with the defendant in this case?" Deborah glanced down at a legal pad on the table in front of her.

"Yes. Her husband was the plaintiff in a case I defended last year."

"As I understand it, that's why she targeted you for poisoning." She flipped a page on her legal pad and jotted a few words.

"That's correct. The insurer I represented refused to pay her husband's claim for benefits. The claim was worth over a million dollars for a medical procedure that the insurer deemed experimental and consequently a noncovered benefit."

"What was the outcome?"

"Her husband died soon thereafter because they couldn't afford to pay for the procedure without the benefit of insurance."

Deborah tapped her pen on the pad, then continued. "Why do you think she held you responsible? It wasn't your decision to deny coverage for the treatment. You were just the defense attorney."

"I've thought about that long and hard." Charles frowned. "To be honest, I'm not certain. Maybe because I was the face she attached to the insurer."

"I can see from her file that Jamie was pretty relentless in her attempts to poison you."

Charles grimaced. "Yes, as I learned in retrospect."

"Let's start with the attempt at the Nasher Sculpture Center which happened March of last year. Detective Gonzales's report states that you never saw her at the event."

He nodded. "That's correct."

"So somehow, the ketamine intended for you ended up in a woman's glass of wine instead of yours?"

"Yes, that's my understanding, too." Charles

swallowed.

"The detective's report also states that you didn't see Jamie Simon in June of last year at The Adolphus Hotel the day the hotel employee was poisoned." Deborah stared at him, as if she expected a different answer.

"That's also correct."

"As you are aware, we're forbidden to use her confession to the police because of the Miranda warning screwup. That doesn't mean we don't know what she said." Deborah pointed her pen at Charles. "That's why it's critical that you testify about her confession to you on the cruise ship. We know she told you everything."

He nodded. "I understand."

She flipped two pages forward and one page back. "Detective Gonzales's report indicates he contacted you when you got home from your cruise in February of this year and inquired whether or not you had remembered anything else relevant to the ketamine poisoning cases. I assume that's accurate?"

"Yes."

"Why didn't you tell the detective about your conversation with her," she said as she leaned forward, "that occurred on the last day of your cruise in early January?"

"Listen, Ms. Brannon, I was honest with Detective Gonzales. He asked if I recalled *anything* on the cruise that I'd forgotten to tell him about the case. When Jamie told me on board that she was responsible for the poisonings, that was the first time I knew about it. It was not something I knew earlier and then forgot about."

"Then why didn't you volunteer the information?" She took off her glasses and scowled at him. "Don't you think it may be useful to the police in solving these serious crimes?"

Charles sighed. "In hindsight, I probably should have disclosed the information. Quite frankly, I thought she had suffered enough. From my conversation with her, I was convinced she was not going to continue with these poisonings."

Deborah shook her head, then arched one eyebrow. "Then why did she steal ketamine from her employer when she returned from her trip?"

Charles did not respond.

"Fine. Mr. Pierce, I want you to focus very carefully on the conversation you had with Jamie about the poisonings. Was it the first time you saw her on board?"

"That's correct."

"You're absolutely sure you never saw her before then?"

"I don't recall seeing her before then." Charles pursed his lips and squinted. "It's possible I did, but I certainly didn't identify her. In fact, I didn't recognize her when she approached my table the last day on the cruise."

"Okay. Start at the time she approached your table. How did it all play out?"

"She addressed me by my name and asked if she could sit down." Forearms stretched outward, Charles shrugged. "That initially surprised me since I hadn't recalled meeting her during the cruise. I was wondering how she knew my name."

"What happened next?"

"She took a seat across from me and asked if I recognized her. I told her something to the effect that while she did look familiar, I couldn't place where I had met her before. She brought up the trial that involved her husband's denied insurance claim. That's when I finally did recognize her." Charles paused.

"Is that when she told you that she had made contact with your wife," Deborah said, "and told her that you and she were having an affair?"

The palms of his hands turned clammy, as they did when he got upset. "Yes. I take it that was in her confession to the police?"

"Yes, Mr. Pierce."

He leaned back in his chair. "Ms. Brannon, I was devastated when my wife committed suicide. I don't want to have to relive that experience. Will we have to go into all that at trial?"

She set her pen down and stared at Charles. "I can't promise you I won't go there. It will be my judgment call during trial. If I feel it's necessary to get the conviction, then I'll have no choice but to ask you about all the details surrounding your wife's death."

"I understand, Ms. Brannon."

"Was this when she confessed to trying to poison you?"

"Yes. As I recall, this was the moment she pulled out an empty vial from her purse and set it on the table. She told me she previously had enough ketamine in the vial to kill a throng of people. I remembered it was ketamine that was used in the poisonings in Dallas. Then I said something like, 'So you poisoned the young man at The Adolphus Hotel?'"

"What did she say then?" Deborah said.

"It was very chilling. In a callous tone, Jamie said I only had to take one sip of the spiked drink and I would've been dead instead of the young man." He shivered.

"Did she mention any other attempts to poison you?"

"Yes an incident at the Water Grill when I was having dinner at the bar with a friend. She had two glasses brought over that were spiked with—"

"Did she specifically mention the Water Grill?"

"Yes. She brought it up."

She jotted another note. "Go on, Mr. Pierce."

"I asked her if she had tried to poison me on board. She said this was the reason her bottle was empty. I then asked her why she was telling me now that she had attempted to poison me." He swallowed. "She said she was tired and wanted me to know I had ruined her life. She then surprised me by saying she was sorry that her actions might have contributed to my wife's suicide."

"Anything else?"

"Yes. I asked her why she wasn't concerned about me telling the police what she had done. She said for me to do whatever I wanted, that she no longer cared."

Deborah jotted some notes. She then said, "Did you tell anyone about her confession to you?"

"Not a soul."

"Why not?"

"I considered informing the ship's security, but then I thought the better of it."

"Why did you reconsider?"

"I had reported some issues to them throughout the cruise. I didn't think they would believe me."

"I assume none of these issues had anything to do with Jamie."

"That's correct. They were completely unrelated to her."

Deborah stared down at her legal pad for a few moments. "I think I have all I need, Mr. Pierce. Do you have any questions for me?"

"Yes, is there a date set for the trial?"

"One week from this coming Monday. I need you to be on call the next day. We will give you as much notice as possible."

"Okay, Ms. Brannon." Charles stood up. "Have a good day."

"You, too, Mr. Pierce."

As Charles rode down the elevator, he could think of nothing but the prospect of having to relive the events surrounding his wife's suicide. How would he ever come to terms with what that Simon woman had done?

CHAPTER 12

Being old school, Charles enjoyed starting every day with a cup of coffee and the *Dallas Morning News*. Each morning, he was always grateful to see the newspaper lying just outside his apartment door.

Charles poured a mug full of coffee and retired with the newspaper to his favorite Eames-designed leather chair, which was situated beside a bank of plate glass windows overlooking Klyde Warren Park and downtown Dallas. His apartment was miniscule but had a million-dollar view. Charles always paused a moment to enjoy the view before cracking open the morning newspaper. It was a beautiful Monday sunny morning.

He separated the various sections before the headline in the Metropolitan News section caught his eye. It read:

BODY FOUND NEAR THE TRINITY RIVER

Yesterday morning, a jogger on his morning run along the Trinity River Trail discovered a man's body lying in the weeds nearby. The corpse was in an area located immediately behind several businesses that front Levee Street on the outer fringe of the Dallas Design District.

A Dallas police spokesperson said the body appeared to be of a fifty- to sixty-year-old white male and had a deep wound to the back of the head. The police indicated the wound does not appear to be self-inflicted and are investigating the matter as a possible homicide. No weapon was found in the area where the body was discovered, nor was any identification.

Businesses located near where the body was discovered are being asked to check their outdoor surveillance cameras to see if anything was captured on video. Police are asking anyone with information to please contact 911.

Wow, that has got to be close to the Trinity River Gallery!

* * *

AS WAS HIS USUAL practice, Charles pulled up to the Trinity River Gallery at 2:00 p.m. and parked right in front of it. When he entered, Sam met him at the door. "You just missed all the excitement."

"Really! What did I miss?"

"A body was found yesterday behind the gallery near the Trinity River Trail. Two police officers were just here."

Charles grimaced. "That's tragic. I read about the incident in the newspaper this morning. The article caught my eye as soon as I opened the paper. What did they have to say?"

"It's a possible homicide case. The victim was apparently struck from behind.

"Yes, that was in the article," Charles said with a nod. "Do the police have any leads yet?"

"Well, they questioned whether we had any external security cameras that might have captured some video of what happened."

"Do you?"

"Only out front above the two front doors. We checked the recording, but there wasn't anything, really. The cameras are aimed at the area immediately surrounding each door. They picked up the blur as a few cars drove past on Levee Street, but nothing else."

"That's too bad," Charles said. "There's something sinister about this area."

Sam gave him half a smile. "As I always say, this is a bohemian neighborhood."

Frowning, Charles pursed his lips. "I think a dead body qualifies as something a little beyond bohemian."

"You're right, of course." Sam sighed. "Let's change the subject. You have any exciting new creations started in Studio 1?"

"I'm in the middle of a new series of paintings all

involving abstract, decaying cityscapes. I think this neighborhood is starting to influence my paintings. Why don't you pop in at the end of the day, and I'll show you what I've been up to lately?"

"Does the invitation come with a glass of wine?"

"Absolutely! You can't appreciate art without wine."

"I'll be there."

Charles made his way through the gallery and back to Studio 1. He wondered how he got so lucky to have his studio in an art gallery. Sam scheduled a new exhibition roughly every month. Sometimes she held group shows of emerging artists, and other times, she scheduled solo exhibitions of more experienced artists. Charles drew inspiration daily by observing the various works of others. He unlocked his studio, turned on some electronic music, and prepared for an afternoon of painting.

At 4:45 p.m., he cleaned his last brush and paused to stare at the progress he had made that day. Satisfied with his work, he pulled out a bottle of Sonoma-Cutrer Chardonnay from his refrigerator. He popped the cork, poured himself a glass, and settled on the couch. He was just finishing off his glass when Sam appeared at the entrance of Studio 1.

"Is the bar still open?" she said.

He stood up. "For my landlady, it's *definitely* open. White or red?"

Sam thought a moment. "Do you have a nice Cab already opened?"

"No, but that doesn't make a difference. How about this HALL Cabernet?"

"You sure you don't mind opening a new bottle?"

"Not at all. What you don't finish today, you can finish tomorrow."

Charles uncorked the Cabernet Sauvignon and poured a glass for Sam, then set the bottle down on his coffee table. "By the way, I actually have something to celebrate. There's a new boutique hotel opening in the Cedars. The hotel, which is cleverly called The Cedars Hotel, put out a call for artist submissions. I submitted several of my paintings from the *Burnt Orange Figurative* series. Believe it or not, the hotel selected two of them for its rooftop lounge area. The cool thing is that all the artists that have been selected are invited to a reception this Thursday evening."

"I assume you're attending?" Sam winked at him. "There will probably be some adult beverages served."

"I haven't decided yet. The invitation said I could bring a guest. I don't suppose you would have any interest in going, would you?"

Sam smiled. "Sure, I'll be happy to be your date."

"No, it's not like that." He shook his head. "I get it that you're already in a relationship with Simone. Let me see if the hotel will let me bring two guests instead of one."

"No need to bother, Charles." She waved her hand in front of her face, as if shooing a fly. "Simone wouldn't be interested in going, anyway."

"Really! Why do you say that?"

"Well, I'm sure a lot of beautiful people will be there, making beautiful people small talk." She crinkled her nose. "Simone absolutely detests those kinds of events."

"But you're okay with it?"

"I *have* to be. I own an art gallery. I deal with these people all the time. Besides, I think it will be fun—and, of course, free adult beverages."

Charles grinned. "I hope the adult beverages are free."

"What time does it start?" Sam glanced at her watch.

"At 8:00 p.m. You want to just meet me in the lobby then?"

"Perfect."

Sam's phone chimed. "Excuse me, Charles, I need to take this." She rose to her feet and exited Studio 1.

Charles finished his glass and recorked both bottles of wine. He thought it was time to head to his apartment. Charles pondered what he was going to have for dinner. He locked his studio and walked through the gallery to the front. Before leaving, he stuck his head in the door of Sam's office and got her attention. She was still on the phone but gave him a wave goodbye.

Why did I invite Sam to the reception? The last thing I need is for another woman I hardly know to hate me enough to kill me.

CHAPTER 13

On Wednesday, Charles pulled up to the Trinity River Gallery a few minutes before 2:00 p.m. Three cars were parked in front. He recognized Mary's and Sam's cars. The third car was a dark, nondescript, Buick sedan. Wondering if the gallery had some visitors, he opened the door and walked inside.

Mary appeared at the opening to the back of the gallery. "Hi, Charles. I was just back at your studio."

Charles's face lit up. "Hi, Mary. I saw a car out front. Please tell me you were showing my art to some rich collectors with tons of disposable income."

"No, sorry."

"Damn it!" he said with a grin, as he walked toward her. "I knew that would be too good to be true."

"Well, I did let someone into your studio, though."

He stopped. "Seriously?"

"Yes. It was that detective who came in here the other day to see you."

"Detective Gonzales?"

"He gave me his card." She peeked down at it. "Yes, that's him."

Charles glanced in the direction of his studio.

"How long has he been here?"

"He just got here and inquired if I knew when you were coming in. I said you're usually here around 2:00 p.m. He asked if he could wait for you in your studio, so I unlocked it and let him inside. I hope that was okay."

"Sure, Mary. He must have some news about that old case I told you about, where I have to testify next week."

When Charles walked into his studio, Detective Gonzales stood near the far wall, examining one of the paintings hanging there. "What do you think about that abstract work, Detective?"

"I haven't made up my mind yet, Pierce." He spun toward Charles. "I do have one question about it, though."

Charles walked up to stand next to him. "What's that?"

"How do you know when it's done?"

"Good question." Charles shrugged. "I guess the artist never knows. At some point, he or she just lays the brush down and decides the painting is done."

"I guess that's why I became a detective instead of an artist. I like more certainty in knowing when I've finished a task."

Charles laughed. "Well, I can appreciate your perspective. That's similar to when I practiced law as a litigator. I either won the case or lost it. I'm assuming, though, Detective, you didn't come here to discuss art."

"That's correct, Pierce. Mind if I sit down?"

"Please have a seat."

Detective Gonzales settled into one of the guest chairs, and Charles sat in the chair across from him. "Are you aware," the detective said, "a man's body was found a few yards from here near the Trinity River Trail?"

"Yes. I read about it in the newspaper. The police were also here earlier, inquiring about the gallery's external video camera."

"Well, we think we recovered the weapon used. A few yards away from the body, an officer discovered a mound of dirt covered with leaves and twigs. Buried about a foot down was a pipe wrench. It had blood on it. Forensics is checking to see if it matches the victim's."

Charles scrunched his eyebrows. "Why are you telling all of this to *me*?"

"I was getting around to that." Gonzales leaned forward. "As the officer was digging through the mound of dirt, he came across one of your business cards."

"Seriously?" Charles looked away, then back at the detective. "You don't think *I* am in anyway connected to that, do you?"

"I *definitely* think you're connected. See, the pipe wrench used to bash in the head of that poor bastard was the same kind as the batch stolen a few months ago from The Home Depot—to be more specific, the same Home Depot where another one of your business cards was found."

Charles shook his head. "Detective, I don't pretend to know anything about forensics, but there have got to be thousands of pipe wrenches similar to the one used in this crime."

Detective Gonzales grimaced. "No doubt about that. However, there's only one Charles Pierce who works out of Studio 1 in the Trinity River Gallery, and your card was found at both The Home Depot burglary and the homicide."

"That's crazy." Charles jolted as if someone had poked him in the eye. "You're not implying I committed these crimes, are you?"

"No, Pierce." He tilted his head forward and twisted his mouth up on one side. "If I thought that, I would've arrested you by now. I do, though, need your help in piecing this puzzle together."

Charles let out a long exhale. "Okay, Detective."

"I have to find out why your business cards keep ending up at crime scenes. Did the same culprit plant your card at both of them? If so, did he think we would conclude you committed both crimes and then were stupid enough to leave your business card?" He snorted. "That's too amateurish and obvious."

Gazing at the floor, Charles was thoughtful for a moment. "On the other hand, maybe the crimes are unrelated." He looked up at the detective. "Yes, my card was at both scenes, but that doesn't mean the same person committed both crimes. There are probably a hundred or so of my business cards floating around out there in Dallas County alone. I'm constantly restocking my card holder after every event."

Detective Gonzales mulled over Charles's assessment. "You're forgetting the pipe wrench. If it matches the ones stolen from The Home Depot, then it must be the same person."

"Can your forensics department conduct any kind of tests to tie the pipe wrench to the burglary?"

"They're looking into it." The detective narrowed his eyes and stared at him. "What is it about you, Pierce?"

"What do you mean?"

"First, Jamie Simon tries to poison you, and now someone is apparently trying to pin a murder rap on you. I could better understand it if you were a prosecutor or criminal defense attorney and dealt with criminals in your profession. But you didn't."

Charles feigned a smile. "No, Detective, I'm just a retired insurance defense attorney trying to be a decent artist."

"Think hard. Has anyone threatened you or caused you to be uncomfortable in the last several months?"

"To be honest, there's one guy who comes to mind."

"Go on."

"During one of the gallery events, a guy walked into my studio. He was poorly dressed and unkempt in appearance. I could smell cigarette smoke and whiskey on his breath. He appeared a bit jumpy."

"What did he do?"

"Before I could say anything, he slid the door to my studio shut. That's when I became nervous. He asked if my name was Pierce. I said that it was and asked if I could help him. This is where it got really bizarre. He said something to the effect that I was the bastard who had gotten his family in trouble."

Detective Gonzales squinted again as he tried to comprehend what Charles was saying. "This guy accused you of getting his family in trouble?"

"Those might not have been his exact words," Charles said as he nodded, "but that definitely was the gist of it."

"What happened next?"

"Fortunately, Sam peered through a crack in the door. Right away I told her to come in, so she slid the door open. This spooked the guy, and he hustled past Sam and out of my studio."

Charles's eyes lit up. "Wait a minute! I remember something else. On his way out, he grabbed a bunch of stuff off that shelf." He gestured toward the shelf next to his door. "The man trashed the hallway outside my studio with shredded magazines and my business cards."

"And you're sure you'd never seen him before that night?"

Charles shook his head. "Not to my recollection."

"How old was this guy?"

"I'm terrible with guessing ages, but I would say late twenties or early thirties." He shrugged. "As I said earlier, he was very unkempt and scruffy-looking. He could have been older."

"The gallery owner got a look at him as well? Had she seen him before?"

"No, Sam said she didn't believe he had ever been here before."

"I take it you haven't seen him again."

"No, that's not correct. I caught sight of him one more time but at a distance."

"When did this occur?"

"A few weeks ago, at another gallery event."

"What happened?"

"Well, the night was going as usual for these types of events. I had a steady stream of people visiting my studio throughout the evening. Then toward the end, I got a phone call from some guy."

"What did he say?"

"He asked me if I was in my studio that night. When I said yes, he hung up. A woman named Lynn had just arrived in my studio, and we struck up a conversation. We were sitting on my couch. Pretty much out of the blue, she kissed me. Then she walked over and slid my studio door closed. When Lynn returned to the couch, she actually mounted me and started aggressively kissing me."

Detective Gonzales smirked. "I bet you put up quite a resistance, Pierce."

Charles twisted in his chair. "Believe it or not, I *did*. I insisted we should return to the gallery. We both got up and exited my studio. I stopped to lock the door. Lynn's cell phone chimed. When I looked around, she was already at the end of the hallway walking toward the gallery while staring down at her phone."

"Did you keep pace with her?"

"No, because then her walk turned into a stride. I tried to catch up with her, but she just quickened her pace toward the front door of the gallery. Before Lynn could exit, I called out and asked her if she was okay. However, she ignored me and left."

"What did you do then?"

"I followed her to the doorway and looked outside. The woman approached a waiting car. When she opened the door to the passenger seat, I got a brief glimpse of man's face from the interior car lights. The car spun away from the gallery."

"Was this the same guy who had threatened you earlier?"

"Yes. It took me a bit, but I remembered that he was the one who had confronted me about getting his family into trouble."

"You sure it was the same guy?"

"I'm positive."

Detective Gonzales scratched his head. "I'm guessing the man was using her to lure you outside."

"Yes, those were my thoughts as well."

"You still have no idea what he meant by you getting his family into trouble?"

"I can't fathom what he could possibly mean."

Detective Gonzales snickered. "You haven't been messing around with this guy's old lady, have you?"

Charles frowned. "Of course not."

"Okay, Pierce. Anything else?"

"One last thing. I assume you know the Jamie Simon case starts next week?"

"Yeah, I heard you agreed to testify for the prosecution."

"Did I have a choice?"

"Probably not. Let me know if you think of anything else about this mystery guy who threatened you. I'll tell you if I find anything else out on my end."

"All right, Detective."

Charles slumped in his chair. *Am I a villain magnet or what? Where is all this involvement with crime going to end?*

CHAPTER 14

On Thursday, at 8:00 p.m. on the dot, Charles pulled his FIAT Spider up to the valet at The Cedars Hotel. A valet took his car, and a doorman opened the front door of the hotel for him.

Charles surveyed the lobby as he walked through it. It was sparsely crowded, although a small group waited to take the elevator up to the rooftop lounge. Charles surmised most people would take advantage of the rooftop bar and stellar views of downtown Dallas he had read about prior to its opening.

He decided to find a seat and scope out the crowd while waiting for Sam to arrive. She had texted him in the car that she was en route but would be running a few minutes late. The crowd was what he had expected to see, part beautiful people and part artists. Some of the attendees were both.

After about ten minutes, Sam walked into the lobby. He stood and waved at her. She spotted him, and they met in the middle of the room.

She said, "This is kind of a funky-looking lobby."

Charles had not checked out the décor yet, since he had been fixated on the crowd. "You're right. Everything seems to be intentionally mismatched." He gestured at the reception desk. "I like the art they positioned behind the desk."

"Yes, it seems to fit. By the way, where did you say your art was placed?"

"The email I received said it was in the rooftop lounge next to the bar." He pointed one forefinger toward the ceiling.

"Well, then, let's go take a look."

They stood side by side until they boarded the elevators and rode to the top floor. When the doors opened, a roar rose from the crowd mingling in the lounge and bar area.

"I assumed most of the crowd would be up here," Charles said. "There's supposed to be some killer views of downtown."

A server came by and gave them both a glass of champagne.

"Okay," Sam said, "where are your paintings?"

"Let's check in the back of the lounge." He motioned with his champagne glass. "There they are, hanging directly opposite from one other."

Sam turned to him and smirked. "You got prime placement in that intimate area there."

"I'm not sure it's prime. People most likely drift back here to be alone. I doubt if checking out the art is first and foremost on their minds."

Sam laughed. "Well, you got *paid*, didn't you?"

"Yes, I did, and of equal importance, I get to list the hotel as a collector in my *curriculum vitae*."

"Let's go check out the cityscape by the pool."

"Are you inspecting the views of downtown or the

beautiful people?"

Sam smiled. "Both, Charles."

After taking in the scenery, they retreated downstairs to the lobby bar for a final drink. They located a table next to the window, and each ordered a glass of wine.

"I've been meaning to ask you something," Charles said. "If you're permitted to tell me, what did the CDADA board decide to do with Cindy Stapler, the managing director who took the money from the association?"

"Believe it or not, they decided to contact the police about the incident. She was arrested for theft."

"Wow, that's an about-face. When I met with the directors about the tax issue, they were all about forgiving her."

"That's true. I think when everything sunk in, the directors got upset. Do you remember John Foxton with the Foxton Heller Gallery? He persuaded the other directors we should turn the matter over to the police. Personally, I abstained from voting on the matter."

"As far as you know, has she gone to trial?"

"I don't know."

"The prosecution will need someone to testify to prove the state's case."

"Maybe John agreed to testify," Sam said. "I really don't know."

Charles took a drink of wine. "Did Cindy ever repay the association?"

"Not yet."

"Then the association still has a tax issue with the IRS to worry about."

"We understand."

Charles smiled. "All I need to know is that I'm *not* part of it."

"Anyway, Charles, I'm glad you invited me to meet you here," Sam said. "It's been fun."

"I appreciate you coming. By the way, what's Simone doing this evening?"

Sam frowned. "I may as well tell you. Simone and I have broken up."

"I'm so sorry, Sam. How long were you guys together?"

"Just about fifteen years. I'm moving out the end of next week. I've leased a small apartment in Oak Lawn."

"Does Simone own the house where you both lived?"

"We own it fifty-fifty. She's going to get a loan to pay me half of the current value."

"That's tough. I know from experience that losing your significant other can be devastating."

"Did you and your wife get a divorce?"

Charles grimaced. "No, she committed suicide. I had just retired from practicing law and was being my usual jerk. That, coupled with the fact she mistakenly thought I was having an affair, pushed her over the edge."

"I'm so sorry, Charles."

"Thank you. What about you and Simone?"

"Well, it's been a long time coming. Simone is distrustful of everything I do. When I mentioned you had rented studio space at the gallery, she even accused me of going over to the dark side."

Charles furrowed his eyebrows. "What exactly does 'going over to the dark side' mean?"

"Simone meant it as going straight."

"Oh, I see. I assume you corrected her?"

"It wouldn't have done any good. She was just looking to pick a fight." She peeked at her phone. "Well, Charles, I better be going. I've a long day tomorrow."

"Me, too. I'll walk out to the valet stand with you."

The valet pulled up Sam's car first. Charles wondered if she was going to give him a kiss. Instead, she handed the valet a five-dollar bill and turned to glance at Charles. "Thanks again. Have a good evening."

"You as well."

The valet pulled up Charles's Spider and had a little difficulty getting out of the car. He said, "Man, that car drives low to the ground."

"Yes, it does. It feels like I'm lying down when I'm in the front seat. But I have to admit, it's a lot of fun to drive."

Charles drove through the heart of downtown Dallas on his way back to his apartment. A block from home, he accelerated to make the traffic light by Klyde Warren Park. The light turned red as he was midway through the intersection. A black SUV behind him accelerated and ran the red light.

Wow, that guy's in a hurry!

He turned left on McKinney Avenue and watched in his rearview mirror as the black SUV did as well. Charles slowed to turn left into the driveway in front of his apartment, which led to the parking garage. He pondered whether the person behind him was a resident as well. Activating his fob, he waited as the garage door crawled upward.

Is that car following me?

The SUV idled a few yards behind Charles's Spider and then reversed and headed back down McKinney Avenue the way it had come, its tires squealing as it sped off. He eased his car through the parking garage to his reserved space on the third floor.

Charles sighed. He was thankful to be home. Not just home, but home *alive*.

CHAPTER 15

Friday morning, Charles had just finished break-fast when he received a call from Deborah Brannon's office directing him to be at the court-house at 2:30 p.m. on Tuesday. He was to wait out-side of the 44th District Court.

The trial had begun the previous day. Charles presumed the first day of the trial had consisted of the voir dire, where the attorneys questioned the prospective jurors. The prosecuting attorneys would attempt to select those jurors they thought would favor the state, and the defense attorneys would select those they perceived would favor the defense. From his prior experience defending insurance com-panies, Charles knew the voir dire to be a tedious and laborious process.

At 2:15 p.m., Charles walked down the hallway toward the 44th District Courtroom. The hallway was lined with wooden benches where jurors and prospective jurors would sit when not in court.

As he arrived at the entrance to the courtroom, the doors were shut. He peeked through the small window in one of the doors. The judge sat on a bench opposite the doors. The jury was impaneled, and no one appeared to be on the witness stand. Deborah

Brannon stood behind the state's table, addressing the court. Charles took a seat on one of the hallway benches.

Ten minutes passed, and then the door to the courtroom opened. The bailiff shouted, "Charles Pierce!"

Charles thought it odd that the bailiff felt the need to shout his name since he was the only person within a few yards of the entrance. He said, "That's me."

After Judge Peter Anderson swore him in, Charles glanced over at the defense table. This was the first time he had seen Jamie Simon since she had confessed to him on the cruise that she had tried to poison him on numerous occasions. She was dressed in a smart two-piece, charcoal-gray pantsuit. Her hair was a natural gray that accentuated her ice-blue eyes, which were focused upon Charles.

Jamie Simon's legal counsel, a man named John Darrow, had quite a reputation and was known as 'Pit Bull Darrow' in the criminal law community, since he could be very tenacious in going after the state's witnesses. He took the accepted legal counsel role of representing clients to the extreme.

Charles checked out the composition of the jury, which comprised six women and six men. He wondered which were selected as favorable for the state and which for the defendant.

Deborah began the direct examination for the state. She asked Charles the usual questions to prove his identity and qualifications. Over the course of the next hour, she had him flesh out all the specifics he could recall about Jamie's confession to him on the last day of his cruise. She spent a great deal of time focusing on the immediate circumstances that led up to the confession.

From his own trial experience, Charles wondered why the counsel for the defense rarely objected to Deborah's questions. If for no other reason, the defense counsel's usual strategy was to object in an effort to disrupt the prosecutor's timing or train of thought.

Deborah paused. "Your Honor, I pass the witness."

Darrow shuffled some papers on his desk as if searching for something. Charles suspected it was all show for the benefit of the jury.

"Mr. Pierce," Darrow said, "I understand from your testimony that you're an attorney, is that correct?"

Charles nodded. "Yes, that's correct."

"Are you still practicing?"

"I've kept my license active, but I only do *pro bono* work now."

"What area of the law did you practice?"

"I represented health insurance companies."

"By representing health insurance companies is how your and Mrs. Simon's paths first crossed, is that correct?"

"Yes, as I testified earlier, she was the wife of a plaintiff who sued my then-client, Mutual Indemnity

Insurance Company."

"You also testified earlier that you won that case. And as a result, Mrs. Simon's husband died, is that right?"

"Objection, Your Honor," Deborah said. "Mr. Pierce is not an expert witness. He's not qualified to testify as to what caused the death of Mr. Simon."

Judge Anderson said, "Sustained."

Darrow smiled. "Let me rephrase my question. You're aware Mr. Simon died shortly after that trial, correct?"

"Yes."

"How then did you learn about his passing?"

"I read his obituary in the *Dallas Morning News*."

Darrow sighed. "How'd that make you feel?"

Deborah said, "Objection. How Mr. Pierce felt is not relevant to this case."

"Your Honor, I'm just trying to determine Mr. Pierce's state of mind," Darrow said. "He testified just now that he quit his practice right after this case. His state of mind may prove to be relevant to this alleged interaction he earlier testified he had with my client on the cruise ship."

Judge Anderson said, "Overruled. You may answer the question."

Charles swallowed. "I felt very badly about it."

Darrow said, "But you had won the case at trial for Mutual Indemnity Insurance Company. Why would you feel badly?"

Charles hesitated. "I quit practicing that type

of law because I didn't like how the outcome of my efforts as defense counsel affected the lives of some of the plaintiffs."

"So is it fair to say you were sympathetic with Mrs. Simon's plight as a grieving widow?"

Charles shifted in the witness chair. "Yes, that's a fair statement."

Darrow glanced over at the jury. "All right, Mr. Pierce, since quitting your practice, what have you done to occupy your time in retirement?"

"I've become a full-time artist."

"Is this for pleasure, or do you sell your art?"

"I do sell my paintings."

"Do have a website where you display your art?"

"Objection!" Deborah said. "What Mr. Pierce does now as an artist is not relevant."

Darrow said, "Again, this line of questioning goes to Mr. Pierce's state of mind."

"Overruled," said Judge Anderson. "I am going to let him continue. Please answer, Mr. Pierce."

Charles said, "Yes, I have a website."

"Is that website www.CharlesPierceArtist.com?"

"Yes, that's my website."

"I have thoroughly checked your website. You're quite creative, Mr. Pierce. Where do you get your inspiration?"

"Are you asking what inspires my artistic creativity?"

Darrow feigned a smile. "As I understand, artists throughout history have used many means at their disposal for inspiration. Some are dependent on illegal drugs while others are dependent on alcohol. Do you have something you rely upon to inspire you?"

Charles creased his brows. "Neither drugs nor alcohol influence my creative process. I can't really articulate what exactly inspires me. I guess it depends upon the subject matter of a particular painting."

Darrow twirled his pen. "So you don't take drugs or drink alcohol, is that correct?"

Charles squirmed at this line of questioning. "I don't take illegal drugs. However, I do drink alcohol."

"Ever had a problem with your drinking?"

Why is Darrow going down this path? He said, "I've had times in my life where I felt I was drinking too much."

"You testified earlier that this conversation you had with Mrs. Simon was on a cruise. Did you drink alcohol while you were on this cruise?"

"Yes, I did drink."

"Is during the cruise one of those times you felt you were perhaps drinking too much?"

Charles shot a glance over at Deborah to see if she was going to object. She was busy writing on her legal pad and did not look up. When he did not respond, Darrow said, "Do you need me to repeat the question?"

"No, I understand the question. Yes, I felt that I was drinking too much while on the cruise."

"How long was this cruise, Mr. Pierce?"

"About a month."

"I see. Let me ask you this, Mr. Pierce. On these types of cruises, do you have to pay for alcohol each time you order a drink?"

Charles was cognizant that Pit Bull Darrow already knew the answer. He said, "No, all the drinks were complimentary."

"What's your drink of pleasure, Mr. Pierce?"

"I enjoy Chardonnay and vodka."

"I see. Do you ever drink both in the same day?"

"Yes, sometimes."

Darrow leaned back in his chair and stared over at the jury. "Tell me, Mr. Pierce, approximately how many drinks did you have on a typical day while you were on this cruise?"

"It would vary from day to day."

"By vary, do you mean you would have five drinks some days and perhaps ten drinks another day?"

Charles sighed deeply. "Sometimes I would have over five drinks a day, especially those days at sea."

"I would suspect a month-long cruise must have several of those days at sea, is that correct?"

"Yes, we spent several days at sea."

Darrow flipped over a page on his legal pad. "On those days where you consumed an excessive amount of alcohol, I would assume it affected your cognitive ability, correct?"

"Objection, Your Honor," Deborah said. "Mr. Pierce is not an expert witness on the cognitive effects of alcohol on the brain."

"But surely," said Darrow, "Mr. Pierce is capable

of testifying as to what effects the consumption of an excessive amount of alcohol had on his personal cognitive ability."

Judge Anderson said, "Overruled. You may answer the question."

Charles chose his words with care. "I suppose one effect is that it hampers my sleeping."

Darrow squinted at him. "So alcohol hampers your sleeping. I would think sleep deprivation combined with excessive alcohol would also adversely impact your ability to discern what is real or not, as well as what you remember, correct?"

Charles grasped where Darrow was going with this line of questioning. He was trying to prove alcohol consumption had altered Charles's perception of reality. Had Jamie really confessed to Charles, or had he just imagined that she had?

Darrow's smirk morphed into a sneer. "Shall I repeat the question, Mr. Pierce?"

"No, I understand the question. I'm having trouble articulating the impact alcohol has on my brain. I suppose alcohol does dull my senses. However, I seriously doubt it would affect my ability to know what is real or not."

Darrow pounded a fist on the table. "You seriously doubt the consumption of excessive alcohol would affect your ability to know what is real, but you can't say for certain, isn't that correct?"

"Mr. Darrow," said Judge Anderson, "please use proper decorum in the courtroom."

Darrow said, "Sorry, Your Honor." He glanced over at the jury. Their eyes were fixed on him. Pit Bull Darrow seemed confident he had won the battle, and perhaps the war, regardless of Charles's response.

"I have testified to the best of my knowledge what impact my drinking has on my cognitive abilities, Mr. Darrow."

"It is approaching 5:00 p.m.," said Judge Anderson. "How much longer do you anticipate questioning this witness, Mr. Darrow?"

Darrow took a sip of water from the glass in front of him. "I only have a few more questions, Your Honor."

"Please proceed."

"Mr. Pierce, you've testified you only had this one interaction with Mrs. Simon while you were on this cruise, is that correct?"

"That's correct."

"So you were on a monthlong cruise, but you never saw or spoke to her before the last day, correct?"

"I might have seen her but just didn't recognize her."

"How many people were on this cruise?"

"I'm not sure of an exact number. It was probably fewer than a thousand."

"This cruise ship must not have been that large, then, to accommodate so few guests, is that correct?"

"Well, I would say it was midsize for a cruise ship."

"There're only a limited number of public places where one could be, isn't that true?"

"I suppose so."

"What are the odds, Mr. Pierce, that you would only see Mrs. Simon the very last day of a month-long cruise?"

"Objection, Your Honor," said Deborah. "Mr. Pierce is not a statistician or otherwise qualified to speculate about such odds."

"Sustained."

Darrow studied his legal pad for a few seconds. "I think that's all I have for cross-examination, Your Honor."

Judge Anderson said, "You may step down, Mr. Pierce."

Charles stepped down from the witness stand and sat in the client chair next to Deborah.

The Judge then addressed the jury. "That's it, ladies and gentlemen. You're dismissed for the day. Please remember my instructions from earlier this morning that you aren't to discuss this case with anyone. Also, please avoid reading or watching any local news that may pertain to this case. Please be back here promptly at 10:00 a.m. tomorrow." He tapped his gavel. "Adjourned for today."

As soon as the jury exited the courtroom, Deborah leaned over to Charles and whispered, "Why didn't you tell me about your drinking problem?"

Charles whispered back, "I don't have a drinking problem. I did drink too much on the cruise, though. When Jamie wasn't trying to poison me, she was probably observing my excess drinking."

Deborah looked around to make certain no one was in earshot. The courtroom had cleared out. "That must be where Darrow got that information. Very clever angle. We need to do some damage control tomorrow morning."

"I understand."

"You indicated to me when we were preparing for trial that Jamie approached you at lunchtime, isn't that right?"

"Yes, that's correct."

"Had you been drinking before she asked if she could join you?"

"No. Definitely not. I never drink in the…" Charles stopped mid-sentence and grimaced. "That was the last day of the cruise. As we were sailing into Sydney Harbour that morning, the waitstaff was serving champagne to all the passengers. I had a glass."

"Just one?"

"As I recall, I just had one. It could've been two. I was about to say that I never drink in the mornings."

She scribbled on her legal pad. "Okay, let me strategize about this for a while."

"Should I be down here at 10:00 a.m. tomorrow?"

"Please get here at 9:30 a.m. in case I need to run anything by you before redirect."

"I'll be here."

Deborah did not look up from her scribbling.

Charles felt a hard pit in his stomach, twisting his gut until he winced.

CHAPTER 16

The next morning, Charles arrived at the 44th District Court at 9:25 a.m. The door to the court-room was open to let jurors in who were arriving for the trial scheduled to begin at 10:00 a.m. Through the open door, Charles observed Judge Anderson taking care of pretrial motions of other cases.

Before Charles could get comfortable, the all-too-familiar voice of Detective Gonzales said, "Pierce, we need to talk."

"Good morning, Detective."

"Let's go down to the far end of the hallway. I don't want any jurors on this case to overhear our conversation."

Charles followed him down the hall to the other end. The detective turned around to face him and gave Charles a slight shove in the chest. "I heard about your testimony yesterday. What was all that crap about you having a drinking problem? Are you trying to blow this case?"

"I did have a drinking problem when I was on that cruise. Remember, I was under oath. I had to answer the defense counsel's questions truthfully."

Detective Gonzales sneered. "How the hell did the damn attorney know you had a drinking problem?"

Charles scratched his head. "I assume he got that information from his client. She wanted to poison me, so obviously she scrutinized all my actions on the cruise. I'm sure she frequently saw me drinking wine or vodka."

"Damn it, Pierce. We need to win this case!"

"I understand your viewpoint, Detective. Jamie stole ketamine from the veterinarian clinic where she worked. I know you said the veterinarian was reluctant to testify against her old sorority sister, but she still reported the theft to the police. Can't you persuade her to testify?"

"She *has* been subpoenaed to testify. However, you can never bet on the testimony of a hostile witness."

Charles felt somewhat sympathetic for him. "Well, maybe Deborah can do some damage control today."

"She just came out of the courtroom. I suspect she's looking for you now. Let's go."

When they reached the courtroom, Detective Gonzales said, "Wait here. I'll go inside and let her know you're here."

A few minutes later, Deborah, accompanied by Detective Gonzales, emerged from the courtroom. He said to her, "Do you need me for anything?"

"No, Detective, thank you."

Detective Gonzales left and Deborah approached Charles. "All right, Charles, testimony will begin in a few minutes. Just sit tight, and the bailiff will come and get you when it's time."

"Will do. Do we need to discuss anything in

advance?"

She squinted at him. "No. I think I know how I'm going to play this."

* * *

THIRTY MINUTES LATER, Charles was on the witness stand. Judge Anderson reminded him he was still under oath. The judge then looked at Deborah. "Counselor, would you like to proceed with the redirect examination of this witness?"

"Yes, Your Honor. Thank you." She continued. "Mr. Pierce, I want to go back to the precise moment when the defendant approached you on the last day of the cruise. Approximately what time of day would you say that was?"

"Around noon. It could've been a tad later. Regardless, I had just sat down to order some lunch."

"Do you recall what the weather was like on that day?"

"Yes, it was a beautiful day. The ship had just sailed into Sydney Harbour. Many passengers were outside in the morning enjoying the view as the ship slowly cruised into port."

Deborah stared at her legal pad. "When the defendant approached your table, did you immediately recognize her?"

"No, the sun was at her back. At first I could only see her silhouette. She looked familiar, but I couldn't place where I might have seen her before."

"The counsel for the defense suggested yesterday that your drinking might have clouded your cognitive ability to remember what happened during your conversation with the defendant. So let me ask you, were you drinking alcohol at the time that Mrs. Simon approached your table?"

Charles shot a glance over at Jamie. She was staring at the jury. He said, "No, I wasn't drinking."

"So when the defendant confessed she had been trying to poison you, you then were cognizant of what she was saying?"

"Absolutely."

Deborah leaned back in her chair. "Mr. Pierce, yesterday you testified you might have had a drinking problem while on this cruise. Does this drinking problem mean you would typically imbibe alcohol morning, afternoon, and night?"

"No, I don't drink alcohol in the morning."

"Do you recall if you drank excessively the night before the defendant confessed to you?"

"No, I don't think I drank excessively the night before."

"On those occasions when you do drink enough, so much it might impair your state of mind, does it affect you the next day?"

Charles smirked. "No, after I get some sleep, then I don't feel any lingering effects of the alcohol." The same as yesterday, he was puzzled why Darrow had not made any objections to the questions. He deduced Pit Bull Darrow had something up his sleeve.

Deborah jotted on her legal pad and then looked up. "Your Honor, I pass the witness."

Darrow shifted in his chair. "Mr. Pierce, you testified that Mrs. Simon joined you at your table, is that correct?"

"Yes."

"You said it was lunchtime. So did you order any food for lunch?"

"No, I was too upset to eat anything after she confessed to me."

"I see. Did you order anything to drink?"

Charles sighed. "Yes. As I recall, I ordered a Pinot Grigio."

"Did Mrs. Simon order anything to eat or drink?"

Charles struggled to remember what, if anything, Jamie had ordered. "I know she didn't order any food. However, I think she ordered a glass of chardonnay."

"After she confessed to you, did she stand up and leave?"

"No, she showed me the empty vial that used to contain ketamine and then she pretended to put some in my glass."

Darrow raised his voice. "So Mrs. Simon pretended to put something invisible in your glass?"

"That's correct."

"Anyone else see her pretend to put this imaginary substance in your glass?"

"Not that I'm aware."

"Not even your waiter?"

"I don't know. He could sense I was upset about

something because he came over to our table to ask me if I was okay."

"How did you respond to the waiter?"

"I said I was okay and asked him to take my glass away."

Darrow chuckled. "You asked your waiter to take your glass of wine away even though Mrs. Simon didn't *actually* put anything into it?"

"Yes."

"Did you order another glass of wine?"

"Yes."

"Weren't you afraid Mrs. Simon would pretend to put something imaginary in your glass again?"

"Objection, Your Honor," Deborah said. "Defense counsel is badgering the witness."

Judge Anderson said, "Sustained."

Charles realized Pit Bull Darrow had already made his point by asking the question. The objection would not sway the jury.

Darrow continued. "Sometime after all of this make-believe, Mrs. Simon got up and left, is that correct?"

"Yes."

"Did you finish your glass of wine?"

"Yes."

"Did you order another glass of wine?"

"No."

"Did you order another alcoholic beverage?"

Charles frowned. "Yes, I ordered a citron vodka and soda."

"Just one?"

"Yes."

Darrow looked at the judge and said, "Excuse me, Your Honor. May I have a moment to confer with my client?"

Judge Anderson said, "Make it very brief."

Charles watched as Darrow whispered something to Jamie and she whispered back to him.

Darrow said, "Thank you, Your Honor. I have just a few more questions. Mr. Pierce, I want to know a bit more about your drinking problem while you were on the cruise. Ms. Brannon asked you if you drank morning, afternoon, and night, is that correct?"

"Yes."

"Didn't you testify that you never drink in the morning?"

"That's correct."

"Not even the morning when the ship was sailing into Sydney Harbour?"

Charles knew where Pit Bull Darrow was going. He could do nothing but tell the truth. "The crew was serving champagne to the passengers as we sailed into Sydney Harbour."

"Did you have a glass of champagne?"

"Yes."

"Do you recall how many glasses of champagne you had?"

"I either had one or two glasses."

"Could it have been three, perhaps?"

"No, this was a special occasion. I don't usually

drink in the morning."

"So I guess it's fair to say your testimony earlier about never drinking morning, afternoon, and night would not be accurate, correct?"

Charles scowled. "My testimony is accurate in that I usually don't drink in the mornings."

Darrow turned to survey the expressions on the jurors' faces. "Your Honor, I have no more questions of this witness."

Charles was dismissed. Staring straight ahead, he plodded down the center aisle out of the courtroom.

Charles walked the hallway toward the bank of elevators. *What a total disaster! My God, Detective Gonzales is bound to visit me again.*

He pressed the down button. *He's probably already sorry Jamie didn't succeed in poisoning me.*

CHAPTER 17

The morning following his testimony at court, Charles slept in late. He experienced nightmares about drinking and seeing his deceased wife after she committed suicide. Shaken, he dragged into the kitchen and forced himself to down a couple of scrambled eggs and a cup of coffee.

After breakfast, he decided some exercise might lift his spirits. Charles's apartment was located five blocks from one of the city's oldest parks, the Katy Trail, an abandoned railroad track that the City of Dallas had converted to a hiking and biking trail in 2000. In only a short time, the Katy Trail had become a popular place for the hordes of people who resided in the various high-rise apartments and condominiums in the uptown and Oak Lawn areas.

Through trial and error, Charles had discovered the quickest route for reaching the Katy Trail. It required him to sprint across several streets to avoid oncoming traffic and to cut through several parking lots.

At midmorning, the rush-hour traffic in the area had died down to a manageable level. While cars were always in the area due to the proximity to downtown Dallas and the businesses located uptown, there was little foot traffic since it was not pedestrian-friendly. Charles often did not encounter anyone else walking as he made his circuitous way to the Katy Trail.

As he cut through the final parking lot before reaching the sidewalk in Victory Plaza that connected to the trailhead, the sound footsteps at a distance behind him made him pause and glance over his shoulder. A man several yards behind him hesitated, then changed course and walked in a different direction.

Charles continued hiking until he reached the Katy Trail. He enjoyed this part of the trail, which was at one time known as Goat Hill. Even though it was a weekday, the trail was still somewhat crowded with joggers, bicyclists, and walkers. Charles quickened his pace to get a little aerobic exercise.

After half a mile, he reached one of the access points to the trail that was located at the south end of Reverchon Park. Charles opted to leave the trail and enjoy a walk through the park. He could reenter the trail on the opposite end of the park, using one several paths. Charles chose the one that ran next to Turtle Creek.

It was autumn, and the colors of the leaves were just changing. A significant amount of underbrush still lined the creek, giving the park a natural beauty unexpected in an urban setting. When that part of the park reached Maple Avenue, he could either go underneath an overpass or climb some concrete steps to street level and cross the street. Except for joggers, many people elected to climb the steps.

Dimly lit and dank, the underbelly of the hundred-year-old overpass was not a pretty sight. Turtle Creek breached its banks every time it rained hard in Dallas. Debris clung to the overpass's support columns located in a creek caused by a recent storm. From time to time, Charles spotted a homeless person huddled under a blanket. That day, his venture through the underpass was undramatic. When he arrived on the north side of Maple Avenue, a middle-aged woman and her beagle out for a walk met him.

Charles said, "Good morning. Beautiful beagle."

"Good morning," the woman said. "Thank you."

The dog sniffed Charles's shoes. He leaned over and petted the dog on the head. This act excited the beagle, which reared up on its hind legs and placed its front paws on Charles's waist.

He held the dog's tag long enough to read its name. "Ah... your name is Greta. She's not too shy, is she?"

"No, Greta's never met a stranger. Come on, girl, let's go." She tugged on Greta's leash, and they headed toward the tunnel in the direction Charles had just come from.

"Have a good day," he called after them.

"You, too."

Charles decided to access the Katy Trail for the remainder of his walk. He walked up the slight incline that led to one of the access points and paused before stepping on the trail to make sure he was not in the path of an oncoming bicyclist.

Charles walked another mile north on the trail before making a U-turn and heading south again. When he returned to the point where he had first entered the Katy Trail from Reverchon Park, a small crowd of people had gathered around the access point and were staring into the park. As he drew closer, he stopped where the area was cordoned off with yellow tape bearing the words CRIME SCENE DO NOT CROSS.

My God! That's where I just came from.

He said to no one in particular, "What happened?"

"We don't know," a man said without turning to look at him. "The police just arrived and sealed off the area."

Charles waited a bit with the crowd and then decided to continue his walk south on the Katy Trail back to his apartment.

He felt a sense of relief as he entered the apartment building. Once he reached the elevator, he didn't press any button, but instead leaned against the wall and bent forward, propping himself up with both hands clutching his knees. A wave of nausea rippled through his gut and he quivered.

After a few moments, it ebbed. He stood up straight and took a deep breath, then pushed the "up" button.

CHAPTER 18

O nce he showered, Charles felt better after his morning exercise on the Katy Trail. He gobbled down a sandwich, then drove over to the Trinity River Gallery. The parking spaces in front were occupied, so he parked on the street halfway down the block.

He opened the door to the gallery and made his way toward the back. As he passed Sam's office, he paused at the entrance to say hi to her, but her office was empty.

He walked into the rear gallery and found Sam sitting with a couple, engaged in enthusiastic conversation. Charles presumed Sam was telling them about the artist of the painting right in front of them. Sam glanced in Charles's direction before he entered the hallway that led to Studio 1. She gave him a quick wave and then returned to her conversation with the couple.

Charles unlocked his studio and plopped down in the chair in front of his easel. He stared at the canvas resting on it. It reflected the efforts of two weeks of painting. *Today, I'm going to finish it!*

He turned on some music and got right into painting at around 1:45 p.m. After he painted for what he thought was about thirty minutes, he glanced at the wall clock in his studio. It read 4:45 p.m.

Where did the time go?

He set down his brush for a few minutes. Sam appeared at the entrance to Studio 1. "How's it going?" she said

"Great. I'm almost finished with this piece. I've been working on it for two weeks. How's your day been?"

"Pretty good. I made a sale of that new artist from Peru whom we just signed a contract to represent."

"Was it that couple you were visiting with when I came in earlier?"

"Yelp."

"Congrats! Shall we celebrate with a glass of wine?"

"I don't want to interrupt your work, especially since you're on a roll."

Charles smiled. "I'm ready to stop. Just give me a minute to clean up a bit."

They enjoyed a couple of glasses of wine. It was now 5:30 p.m.

Sam said, "That was lovely, Charles. Thank you."

"My pleasure."

She stood up and checked her phone. "I'm out of here. Would you like for me to wait for you before I lock up?"

He shook his head. "I've changed my mind about quitting for the day. I'm going to paint awhile before I leave, now that I'm so close to finishing this piece."

Sam grabbed the empty wine glasses. "I'll put these in the dishwasher before I leave. Then I'll lock you in."

"Thanks, Sam. Have a good evening."

"You too."

Charles squeezed some paint and medium on his palette and mixed them together. He found an appropriate brush and dabbed it in the blended color. After painting for about hour, he set the brush down, satisfied the painting was finished. He felt the effects of the wine, and his right hand throbbed with pain from having clutched the brush for so many hours.

Charles checked the clock. It was 6:30 p.m. He cleaned his palette and brushes and walked through the gallery to the front door. It was already dark outside. Other than the fixture over the door, nothing provided any visible light. The light bulb in the ancient streetlight across the street burned out years ago and had never been replaced.

Charles locked the door behind him and paused to allow his eyes to adjust to the darkness. He took three steps down the sidewalk in the direction of where he had parked his FIAT Spider.

A gunshot fired from somewhere across the street. The bullet sailed right by his head, then shattered the plate glass window of the gallery. Charles tripped and fell flat onto the sidewalk. He was not certain whether he had fallen on purpose out of fear or because he had lost his balance.

Shards of glass from the window cascaded on

top of him. Struggling to regain some composure, Charles lay motionless on the sidewalk between the gallery and a car parked in front.

Another shot rang out, striking the brick next to where the plate glass window had been. Charles felt blood trickling down his back, the result of a shard of glass that had lodged into his flesh. He managed to get his phone out of his pocket and dialed 911.

While tires squealed, he caught a glimpse of the silhouette of a black SUV heading north on Levee Street. Charles hoped the shooter had driven away in it.

Sirens wailed in the distance. As they got closer, he remained horizontal on the sidewalk. Charles did not try to sit up until he caught sight of a patrol car round the corner from Oak Lawn Avenue onto Levee Street. A sharp pain throbbed in his upper back.

The patrol car pulled up and parked in front of the gallery. Two officers exited the car and drew their guns from their holsters before they advanced with great caution.

"Officers," Charles shouted, "I'm over here!"

As they approached him, their heads jerked around while they sized up the area. One of them called out, "Are you armed?"

"No, I'm not armed."

When they got closer, one of the officers pointed his flashlight at Charles, illuminating his face and the immediate area around him. "Did you call 911?" he barked.

"Yes, Officer. I think someone tried to shoot me."

The second officer appeared on the other side of Charles, approaching from the rear. "Are you injured?"

"It feels like my back is cut from one of the shards of glass."

Both officers were now within a few feet of Charles, staring down at him. One of them said, "I'm Officer Daniels, and this is Officer Reid. Who are you?"

"I'm Charles Pierce. Is it okay for me sit up?"

"Go ahead," Officer Daniels said. "Do you need any help?"

"I probably can handle it." Charles flinched in pain but managed to sit up. The back of his shirt was drenched with blood.

Officer Daniels said, "You got any ID?"

Charles squirmed until he was able to fish his wallet out of his back pocket. He removed his driver's license and handed it to Officer Daniels.

He studied it for a moment and then handed it to Officer Reid, who said, "I'll check him out and call EMS." He left and walked back to the police car.

"What happened here tonight?" Officer Daniels said.

"I had finished painting for the night and locked up the gallery. As I walked down the sidewalk in the direction of my car, someone took two shots at me."

"You own this gallery?" He shined the flashlight on the sign over the front door.

"No, I lease an artist studio here. Can I text the

owner about the broken front window?"

"What's his name?"

"He's a woman and her name's Sam Sterling."

After a few minutes, Officer Reid rejoined them. "Nothing on him. EMS will be here in five minutes."

Charles texted Sam about the incident. When he looked up from his cell phone, Officer Daniels said, "You were walking to your car, and someone just started shooting at you?"

Charles coughed. "That's correct."

In a brusque voice, Officer Daniels said, "Did you see anyone?"

"No, although I did see a dark SUV drive away after the shooting stopped."

Officer Reid said, "How many shots were fired?"

"Two. The first shattered the window, and the second ricocheted off the exterior of the gallery."

His tone bordering on terse rudeness, Officer Reid said, "Can you think of any reason someone would use you for target practice?"

Charles hesitated. "There was a guy who threatened me in my studio several weeks ago at a gallery event."

"This guy have a name?"

"I don't know his name, but I told Detective Gonzales about it. He came to my studio concerning an unrelated matter."

The officers glanced at each other. Officer Daniels said, "Okay, we'll check your story out with him."

The EMS ambulance rounded the corner from Oak

Lawn Avenue onto Levee Street and parked next to the police car. Two men in scrubs came running over to Charles. The first paramedic said, "What have we got here?"

"I think my back got cut," Charles said, "from all the broken glass."

The paramedics removed Charles's bloody shirt to examine his back. The other paramedic said, "You've got several pretty significant lacerations. You're gonna need sutures. Do you hurt anywhere else?"

Charles groaned. "Maybe some bumps and bruises from falling on the pavement, but nothing serious."

"We can take you to Baylor or Parkland to get you checked out," the first paramedic said. "Any preference?"

"Baylor. It's in my health plan."

Charles's phone beeped, showing a text from Sam. "Officers," he said, "the owner is en route and should be here in a few minutes."

"Officers, we're going to take him to Baylor," the other paramedic said. "Do you need to ask him anything before we leave?"

"It's okay to take him," Officer Daniels said. "We know how to get ahold of him if we need him."

The paramedics lifted Charles onto a gurney and wheeled him in the direction of the ambulance. Before they reached the back door of the ambulance, Sam arrived and double-parked behind the police car. She jumped out of the car. "My God! Charles, how bad are you hurt?"

Charles forced a smile. "Well, I'm not good, but I'm better than the front window of your gallery. Seriously, I'm okay. I just have some cuts."

"Excuse us, ma'am," one of the paramedics said, "we need to go."

As they loaded Charles into the ambulance, he shouted, "Sorry, Sam! The officers will fill you in."

Holy crap, someone is trying to kill me! He winced as he reached up to wipe the corners of his eyes.

CHAPTER 19

Baylor University Medical Center personnel deemed Charles's wounds as urgent but not requiring emergency care. As a result, it was almost 3:00 a.m. before he was treated and rolled to a room. Charles had a fitful night trying to get some rest. He had to sit up in bed to avoid putting pressure on the wounds to his back.

Later that morning, the attending physician informed Charles he would not be discharged until the following day. Charles wanted to go home but was so tired, he did not put up any resistance to the decision.

That afternoon, at 2:00 p.m., the door to his room opened, and Detective Gonzales strolled inside. "How are you feeling, Pierce?"

Charles switched off the television with the remote. "I've been better. But surely, Detective, you didn't come down here to check on my health."

"I'm sure you don't mind if I sit down." Without waiting for Charles to answer, Detective Gonzales sat in one of the visitors' chairs. "I talked to Officer Daniels, and he filled me in on what happened last night."

"I don't suppose you've arrested the culprit yet,

have you?"

"No arrests have been made, although the officers reported the crime as attempted murder, which
allows forensics to get involved. An officer was able to
get the remnants of a bullet that was lodged into one
of the interior walls of the gallery."

Charles shook his head. "I feel for poor Sam. She
has to deal with a broken window and a bullet buried
in her gallery wall."

Detective Gonzales leaned forward in his chair.
"Officer Daniels says you didn't get a good look at
whoever took a shot at you, but you did see a dark
SUV haul ass after the shooting stopped."

"That's correct."

"You think it might have been the guy who threatened you in your studio?"

"I know of no one else who has shown any animos-
ity toward me."

"You told me earlier, Pierce, you saw a woman
possibly get into this guy's car one time, correct?"

Charles massaged his temples. "Yes, Detective."

"Do you remember what kind of car he was
driving?"

"I only got a glimpse of it."

"Can you say whether or not it was an SUV?"

Charles tilted his head to one side. "No, I'm pretty
certain it was a sedan. It definitely wasn't an SUV."

"I need you to come down to headquarters after
you're discharged from the hospital."

"What for?"

"One of your business cards showed up again near a crime scene."

"You're kidding." He snorted. "*Again?*"

Detective Gonzales scowled. "I don't kid when I'm on the taxpayers' dime. Yesterday your card made an unfortunate appearance near a dead woman's body in Reverchon Park."

Charles straightened up in bed and groaned at the sudden movement. "I was in Reverchon Park yesterday morning!"

"I'm aware of that, Pierce. I'm glad you verified it for me."

"How the hell did you know I was there yesterday?"

"You were caught on security video twice. There's tape of you leaving the Katy Trail at the south Reverchon entrance and tape of you reentering the trail on the north side of Maple Avenue. When I learned your card was found at the scene, I viewed the tapes and identified you."

Charles took a moment to contemplate the detective's words. "That's correct. I was at both places."

The door of the room swung open, and a nurse entered. "Excuse me, gentlemen. I have to take Mr. Pierce's vitals."

Detective Gonzales said, "Do you need me to wait outside?"

"No, you're fine. I'll just be a minute."

The nurse checked Charles's temperature and then took his blood pressure. She sighed. "Your blood pressure is a little elevated. You're 150 over 80."

"I'm not surprised," Charles said, "after the news this gentleman just told me."

"Okay, Mr. Pierce," the nurse said, "I'll leave you two alone now." She left the room.

Charles took a sip of water through a straw in a glass that sat on a side table. "You said my card was found near a dead body?"

Detective Gonzales nodded. "Within a few feet of a woman named Jennifer Colby."

"Did the police recover a weapon?"

"I don't want to get into that at this time."

"Well, can you at least tell me if I'm a suspect?"

Detective Gonzales stood up. "I'm not ready to label you anything at this time. Are you being discharged tomorrow morning?"

"That's my understanding."

"You think you're up to coming down to headquarters tomorrow afternoon?"

Charles frowned. "I'm sure I can manage."

"All right, Pierce, give me a call when you're back home tomorrow, and we'll schedule a time."

"Yes, Detective."

Damn, what's happening? I almost get killed and now I am tied to another murder! He flopped back against the pillow and screeched when the stitches in his back absorbed the impact.

CHAPTER 20

Charles was discharged from the hospital at 10:00 the next morning. He caught a cab to the Trinity River Gallery to pick up his car from two days ago.

The cab let Charles out in front. He considered going inside to visit with Sam but opted to go home instead. He walked, vigilant and hesitant, down the sidewalk to where his FIAT Spider was parked.

God, I hope no one has messed with my car.

Charles heaved a long sigh. His car appeared to be in the same condition as when he had last seen it. He drove the short distance to his apartment. It was now almost noon. He gave Detective Gonzales a call.

Look how my life has changed. I now have a Dallas detective listed among my personal contacts.

Detective Gonzales told him to be at headquarters at 3:00 p.m.

He arrived at 2:45 p.m. and an officer ushered him to an interrogation room. He sat down at the wooden table and checked out the décor. In the middle of the table was a small microphone that was used for recording interrogations, and a camera was mounted near the ceiling focused on the chair where Charles was seated. The walls and ceiling were painted a gray-green color that was so prevalent many years ago in public institutions.

The door opened, and Detective Gonzales and another man entered the room. What was the protocol for those being interrogated? Should he stand up and offer to shake hands? He elected to remain seated.

Detective Gonzales said, "Pierce, this is Detective Grayson."

Detective Grayson, a husky man in his upper twenties with the physique of a linebacker, nodded in the direction of Charles.

"Before we formally get started," Detective Gonzales said, "I need to give you the Miranda warning. You have the right to remain silent. Anything you say can and will be used against you in a court of law. You have the right to talk to a lawyer for advice before we ask you any questions. You have the right to have a lawyer with you during questioning. If you cannot afford a lawyer, one will be appointed for you before any questioning if you wish. If you decide to answer questions now without a lawyer present, you have the right to stop answering at any time."

Never thought I would receive the Miranda warning.

"I understand," Charles said. "Is this being recorded?"

"Yes, all formal interrogations are recorded."

"I assumed that was the case."

"Okay, tell us everything you can remember about

the morning of November 3."

"As you know, I testified in the Jamie Simon case the day before. I didn't sleep well that night and felt like crap the next morning. After breakfast, I walked from my apartment on McKinney Avenue down to the Katy Trail. There's usually a lot of cars and no foot traffic on my route. That morning, though, I heard footsteps behind me when I cut across one of the vacant parking lots. When I looked around, the person who I believed was following me suddenly veered off to the left. I didn't think much of it and continued my route toward the trailhead past Victory Plaza."

Detective Grayson said, "Was this person a man or a woman?"

"A man."

"How close was this man to you when he changed course?"

"I would say about thirty yards."

"Did you get a good look at him?" said Detective Gonzales.

"Not at all."

"Do you recall what time you reached the Katy Trail?"

"Not exactly, but I left my apartment building around 10:00 a.m. It usually takes me about fifteen minutes to reach the trailhead."

"Continue with your story." Detective held out his left hand sideways in front of his chest, using a sweeping circular motion for emphasis.

Charles rested his elbows on the table. "It was a cool, crisp day, so after I walked the trail a bit, I decided to leave it at the south Reverchon entrance. I walked through the park until I reached Maple Avenue. There you have to decide whether to climb the steps to street level to cross the street or take the path next to Turtle Creek and go under the overpass—"

"Did you see anyone in the park before you reached Maple Avenue?" said Detective Gonzales.

"A few people were there. The occasional jogger and people throwing frisbees to their dogs. I didn't see anything out of the ordinary."

"Did you see that guy again," Detective Grayson said, "the one you thought was following you earlier?"

Charles shook his head. "No, not that I am aware of, anyway."

Detective Gonzales said, "Did you speak to anyone while in the park?"

"No."

"Let's go back to the time where you reached Maple Avenue. Tell us what you did."

"I decided I would take the path under Maple."

"Did you encounter anyone while you were under the Maple Avenue overpass?"

"No one was in the tunnel. However, I did encounter a woman and her dog just as I reached the other side of the overpass."

Detective Gonzales leaned forward. "Can you describe this woman?"

"She was Caucasian, in her forties or fifties. To be honest, I remember her dog better than her."

The detectives glanced at each other. Detective Gonzales said, "Why do you remember the dog so well?"

"It was a beautiful beagle. My family had one when I was a kid. I've always liked the breed."

"Go on."

"That's pretty much it. The woman continued south on the path under Maple, and I decided to access the Katy Trail again."

"Was anyone else around," Detective Grayson said, "when you encountered the woman and her dog?"

Charles sighed. "I didn't notice anyone around."

Detective Gonzales said, "Did you have any physical contact with her?"

Charles creased his brows. "No."

"Okay, Pierce, so you then accessed the Katy Trail at the park's north entrance, correct?"

"That's correct. I walked about a mile north on the trail and then made a U-turn and headed back south. When I reached the south access to the park, I noticed a crowd of people staring into the park. I walked over and asked what had happened. Some guy said he didn't know because the police had just arrived and cordoned off the area. I then left and headed back to my apartment."

"Weren't you curious..." Detective Grayson's tone was curt. "...to find out why the police had cordoned off the area?"

"I guess I wasn't curious enough to wait."

"Is that because you already *knew* why the police were there?"

Charles's face flushed with anger. He took two deep breaths and then said, "No, Detective, I had no clue why the police were there." He glared at him. "Listen, do you *really* think I would kill some poor woman and then leave my business card at the scene of the crime? Who would be *stupid* enough to do that?"

"To the contrary, maybe it was a clever move on your part to leave your card. You kill the woman and then leave your card because you know no one would suspect you of doing something so dumb."

"That's ludicrous!"

"Would you be willing," Detective Gonzales said, "to let us take a DNA sample and be fingerprinted?"

Charles eyes widened. "*Now*, you mean?"

"No time like the present." His tone was almost smug.

"All right."

Detective Gonzales said to Detective Grayson, "Go get a technician to administer the DNA sample and the prints." To Charles, he said, "This will only take a few minutes."

"You don't really believe," Charles said to Gonzales, "I had anything to do with this, do you?"

"All I can say so far, Pierce," the detective said as he scrunched up one side of his mouth, "is you have an uncanny knack for being connected in some way to a lot of crime."

"Do you know how this woman was killed?"

"Blunt trauma to the back of her head."

"That's horrific! What was the weapon?"

Detective Gonzales stared at Charles but did not answer.

Detective Gray returned with a technician who fingerprinted and took a DNA sample from Charles.

Detective Gonzales said, "Okay, Pierce, that's all for now. You're free to go."

"What happens next?" Charles said as he pushed back his chair.

"We wait for forensics to do their thing. I'll be in touch."

Charles got up to leave, and Detective Grayson opened the door for him. Before exiting the room, Charles said, "Detective Gonzales, how did the Jamie Simon case play out?"

He scowled at Charles. "She walked, damn it!"

"I'm very sorry."

"You better watch your ass, Pierce," Detective Gonzales grumbled. "Besides someone trying to shoot you, Jamie Simon may be back on the warpath, trying to poison you."

"That's such a pleasant thought," he said, his tone awash in sarcasm. "Thanks, Detective."

When he exited police headquarters, Charles felt a lump in his throat. He hurried to his car, glancing over his shoulder every few seconds.

CHAPTER 21

Early the next afternoon, Charles decided to go to his studio. While his back was still sore from the wounds he had received, the pain was manageable. He did not feel like painting but thought returning to some type of normality would lift his spirits.

Sam's car was parked in front, and Charles eased his FIAT Spider in the place next to it. The Trinity River Gallery looked completely different with plywood over the opening that the plate glass window had once occupied. He turned the handle to open the door, but it was locked. Sam must have done so out of an abundance of caution. After all, her gallery had been riddled with bullets a few nights ago. Charles fished his keys out of his pocket and unlocked the door.

Sam came out of her office as he was relocking the door from inside the gallery. "Charles, I'm a bit surprised to see you. How do you feel?"

He forced a smile. "A little tender, but I'll live. Listen, Sam, I'm really sorry about your window."

"No worries. Insurance covered almost all of it. In fact, the new window will be installed tomorrow."

"Really? That's pretty quick. I hope it's bullet-proof glass."

Sam laughed. "I see you haven't lost your sense of humor."

"My God, I've had some strange experiences these past few days." Charles gestured with his hands, but grimaced when the movement tugged at the sutures in his back. "First, I get shot at outside the gallery, and then I'm interrogated at police headquarters concerning a body found in Reverchon Park."

"You were interrogated? What was that all about?"

"My business card was found at yet another crime scene. This time, it was near a woman's corpse."

"Did you say 'corpse'?"

Charles rubbed his head. "I'm afraid so. The scary thing is that I was in the area then."

Sam studied Charles's face, as if trying to determine if he were serious. "How do you know you were there at the same time?"

"I even talked to the woman who was killed."

"Charles, I can't tell if you're joking, but you're scaring me."

"Sorry, Sam. Let me explain. I often walk on the Katy Trail for exercise. The morning all of this occurred, I opted to leave the trail to walk a bit in Reverchon Park. At Maple Avenue, hikers are required to either climb the steps to walk across at street level or take the path next to Turtle Creek underneath it. Are you familiar with the area?"

Sam nodded. "Yes, I've been there several times."

Charles described his encounter with the woman and her pet beagle. "When I got back to the south entrance to Reverchon Park, the police had the area cordoned off. Apparently, someone had discovered the woman's body. Video cameras are installed at both the location where I left the trail and where I came back onto it. After Detective Gonzales learned that my card was found, he viewed the videotape and identified me. So that's why I was interrogated."

"Did the police say how she died?"

"Detective Gonzales said blunt trauma to her head. I asked if they had found a weapon, but the detective wouldn't tell me."

Frowning, Sam squinted at him. "Why do you think he wouldn't tell you?"

Charles sighed. "I don't have a clue."

"Did the police say whether they had any other suspects?"

"I think I'm the only suspect, person of interest, or whatever they call someone who's interrogated."

"To change the subject," Sam said, "the police *did* remove a bullet fragment that was lodged in the gallery wall."

Charles smirked. "Maybe they will at least find the guy who shot at me."

"By the way, Simone asked how you were doing."

"Simone? Your ex?"

"Yes, she just called me out of the blue the morning after the shooting."

Charles glared at her. "How did *she* know about the shooting?"

"I don't know. She probably heard it on the news."

"Do you recall *exactly* what Simone said?"

"She told me she heard about the shooting outside the gallery and that a man was injured. I guess she just assumed it was you."

"I've never even met Simone. Why do you think she was concerned it might be me?"

Sam turned aside and shrugged. "Look, Charles, I can't begin to guess why Simone inquired about you." She sounded irritated. "She and I are no longer a couple. I don't know why she called."

"Oh, I apologize, Sam! I'm just a little unnerved about everything that's going on. I feel like my life is in danger, yet the police think I'm a murderer. Am I a victim or a suspect?"

"No need to apologize." Her tone softened. "I understand things are a bit crazy. Are you going to paint today?"

"No, but I'm going into to my studio for a while. I think more for therapeutic reasons than anything else."

"I've got to get back to work," Sam said. "If you're still here in an hour, I'll let you offer me a glass of wine."

Charles grinned. "You've got a date."

Soon afterward, Charles sat in his studio staring at a painting he had begun earlier. He was not in the mood to paint this afternoon. He moved over to the couch, closed his eyes, and dozed off for a few minutes. It had been a trying few days.

Stirring himself wider awake, Charles walked

over to his refrigerator and pulled out a Rombauer Chardonnay. He popped the cork and poured himself a generous glass. He was halfway finished when Sam appeared at the door to his studio. "I can see you started without me."

"For medicinal purposes only, Sam. I have an exquisite Zinfandel if you would like to try it." He pulled the cabinet door open and slid a bottle out.

"Here, let me open that." Sam held out her hand. "After all, you're suffering from your injuries."

Charles laughed. "I have sutures in my back, not my hands. But you're welcome to open it."

With no trouble at all, Sam unscrewed the cork and poured herself a glass.

"Wow!" said Charles. "That's the fastest I have ever observed someone opening a bottle of wine. Obviously that's not the first one you've opened."

"You're right. I bet you didn't know I am a level-two sommelier. One of my many occupations over the years."

"Really?" Charles tilted his head to one side. "Why didn't you stick with that?"

"Art. Owning a gallery has always been my first passion."

Charles leaned back on the couch, flinching a bit. "I keep forgetting about these sutures."

"When will you get them out?"

"In about a week. By the way, are you having a new exhibition before the holidays?"

Sam took a drink of her Zinfandel. "Yes, I'm having

an exhibition on Neorealism. People love this genre of art. Since the gallery is generally dead around the holidays, I wanted to host an exhibition that would entice folks to attend."

"With any luck and a little diligence, I'll have that painting on my easel done by then."

They enjoyed another glass of wine and then decided to call it a day. They left the gallery together. When Sam turned around to lock the front door, a dark-colored car squealed off down Levee Street toward Oak Lawn Avenue. They both spun around.

Sam said, "My God, I think that was Simone!"

Charles recognized the vehicle as a black SUV. "She drives an SUV?"

"She drives a 2017 Subaru Crosstrek."

"She sure seemed in a hurry to get out of here."

"That's Simone." Sam tsked-tsked. "She can be a bit reckless at times. I used to find that charming."

"I'm sorry I never had a chance to meet her."

"I wonder why she was hanging around outside the gallery?" Sam said. "If she wanted to see me, then all she had to do was come inside. Simone is quite a drama queen."

Cognizant that Sam's question was rhetorical, Charles did not respond.

"Have a good evening," Sam said as she walked toward her car. "Are you having another delicious frozen dinner for supper tonight?"

Charles smiled. "No, I think I may whip up a little pasta dish."

"What are you going to have with your pasta?"

"I have this wonderful recipe were I sauté scallops in a white wine sauce and mix them with angel hair pasta."

Sam laughed. "I assume your wine of choice is Chardonnay."

"Of course, but occasionally, I'll use Pinot Grigio."

"That sounds tasty. You'll have to cook for me sometime."

"Anytime, Sam. You'll love my view of downtown Dallas, if nothing else."

Sam got in her car and drove away. Charles sat in his Spider and checked his phone for emails. Finding nothing of interest, he slid it in the cupholder and started the engine. As he was driving the short distance to his apartment, it occurred to him that it was perhaps Simone's SUV he had spotted the night someone had shot at him.

Did Simone try to kill me? But why? This is crazy. I must be mistaken!

He checked his rear view mirror a third time before he turned into the parking garage.

Maybe I should tell Gonzales and his buddy detective that Simone could be the one who shot at me. He paused to let the security gate go up. *Hell, they wouldn't believe me anyway!*

CHAPTER 22

The next afternoon, Charles sat and stared at the canvas on his easel for several minutes. He decided he had finished the painting and glanced at the clock on his studio wall. It was 4:00 p.m.

Charles cleaned his brushes and poured himself a glass of Chardonnay. At a distance, the buzzer sounded in the front of the gallery as it always did when someone entered. He considered opening his studio door in case someone decided to come see the resident artist. Not in the mood for visitors, he opted to remain seated.

After a few minutes, someone knocked on his door. Charles said, "Come in."

The door slid to the side, and Detective Gonzales and Detective Grayson entered his studio.

Right away Charles's palms turned sweaty. In a calm voice he said, "Good afternoon, Detectives."

"I'm afraid it's *not* a good afternoon for you, Pierce," Detective Gonzales said. "We're going to have to arrest you."

Parroting the lines he had always heard in old detective film noirs, Charles said, "Why? On what charge?"

In a gruff tone Detective Gonzales said,

"Homicide."

Charles's emotions shifted from anxiety to anger. "You're accusing me of killing that woman in the park, aren't you? That's completely insane and you *know* it."

Detective Grayson dangled a pair of handcuffs from one hand. "I have to put these on you."

"Really?" Charles's eyebrows shot up. "You have to put me in *handcuffs*?"

"I'm afraid so, Mr. Pierce. It's standard procedure."

"Other than being in the park around the same time the woman was there, what evidence could you possibly have linking me to her death?"

"Before we go any further," Detective Gonzales said, "you know the drill. I have to recite the Miranda warning to you."

The same as when Charles was interrogated earlier, the detective read him his rights. Charles said, "Okay, damn it. I understand my rights. Now could you please tell me what evidence you have for arresting me?"

Detective Gonzales said, "Your fingerprints."

"My fingerprints?" Palms forward, Charles shrugged. "You found my fingerprints on the *corpse*?"

"Your fingerprints were found on the dog's collar."

"But I petted the *dog*, but I didn't touch the *victim*." He held up one finger. "Did you find the weapon?"

"Not yet. But a warrant was issued this morning to search your apartment, car, and studio. I suspect your apartment is being searched as we speak."

Detective Grayson said, "Put your hands behind your back."

Charles complied and was handcuffed for the first time in his life.

What will Sam and Mary think when they see me like this?

The detectives walked behind him through the back of the gallery to the front. Charles's eyes darted back and forth, glancing at the various paintings on the walls. He was cognizant of the art but did not really see it. He felt dazed and helpless.

Sam came to stand at her office door. "Charles, what's going on?"

"We apologize, ma'am," Detective Gonzales said, "for the intrusion into your business."

"So sorry, Sam, for the spectacle in your gallery. They're arresting me for a crime they're perfectly aware I didn't commit." Charles glared at both detectives as they marched him out the front door.

CHAPTER 23

Charles was taken to Lew Sterrett Justice Center, where his handcuffs were removed, and then he was booked and fingerprinted. All of his personal possessions were confiscated and sealed in a paper envelope.

He said to the officer conducting the check-in process, "Doesn't a judge have to formally inform me of the charges filed against me?"

"In due time. Just relax," the detention officer said. "You're not going anywhere soon."

Another officer escorted Charles to a holding cell, a large room with chairs arranged in rows in the middle. The chairs were about one-third occupied. The officer pointed at an empty seat. "Sit in that chair, and do not move unless you are authorized to do so by the presiding officer. If you need to go to the bathroom or get a drink of water, raise your hand."

The presiding officer was an obese man who appeared to be occupying his time by filling in a crossword puzzle. Every now and again, he would raise his head to let his eyes scour the room and then resume his puzzle.

A man two rows in front of Charles raised his hand. He held it in the air at least five minutes before the presiding officer noticed him. The man asked to go to the bathroom, and the officer granted him permission.

How long are they going to keep me here?

Another officer came into the room and handed the presiding officer a piece of paper. He shouted, "John Fisher!"

A young man raised his hand.

"It's your time to be arraigned," the presiding officer said. "Follow Officer Collins."

Officer Collins handcuffed the young man and led him out of the room.

Several hours passed. Every few minutes, Charles checked the clock on the wall. Time passed at a snail's pace, a snail with nowhere to be. By 7:00 p.m. Charles wondered if he would have to spend the night seated in the room.

At long last, at 7:30 p.m., an officer entered the room and handed the presiding officer a piece of paper. The presiding officer shouted, "Charles Pierce!"

Charles raised his hand. The presiding officer instructed Charles in the exact manner as the twenty men who had preceded him.

The other officer handcuffed Charles and led him into what resembled a makeshift courtroom. Charles surmised the courtroom had been devised to expedite the arraignment process. The judge was a middle-aged African-American woman dressed in a traditional black robe. Charles was told to stand and wait until he was called before her.

The judge said, "Charles Pierce."

The officer led Charles to the front of the court-room. The judge did not look up right away. She seemed to be reading some papers in front of her. Then she raised her head and stared at Charles. "Mr. Pierce, I'm Judge Tolbert of the 33rd District Court."

Not knowing whether to speak, Charles remained silent.

She continued. "Under Texas Penal Code § 19.02(b)(3), you have been charged with felony murder. You have knowingly or recklessly caused another person to lose her life. Do you understand this charge?"

"Yes, Your Honor."

The judge said, "I understand you're an attorney."

"Yes, Your Honor. I'm retired."

"This is the part where I inform you of your rights to a public defender if you cannot afford an attorney." She leaned forward. "However, since you're an attorney, is it correct to assume you have the means to hire counsel?"

"Yes, Your Honor. I can afford to hire an attorney."

"According to the law, I am required to set your bail," the judge said. "Under special circumstances, the bail can be limited to personal recognizance. In other words, the only bail you have is your promise to make all required appearances in court. You have no prior criminal record, you're an attorney, and as such, an officer of the court."

Charles held his breath.

"As a result," she continued, "I am going to release

you on your own personal recognizance if you agree to attend all required court appearances. Do you understand and agree?"

Charles exhaled. "Yes, Your Honor. Thank you."

"Personal recognizance is so granted in lieu of monetary bail."

Charles was led back to the check-in officer to recover his possessions. He was free to go.

Taxis were lined up outside of the Lew Sterrett Justice Center, the kind of scene one would expect to see outside of some swanky hotel in downtown Dallas, not outside the jail. Charles debated whether to walk through downtown back to his apartment or catch a ride instead. He was tired and hungry, so he opted for the cab.

Charles wondered what his building manager thought about his premises being searched. It was probably a breach of the leasing agreement to have an apartment subjected to a police search.

He unlocked his front door and hurried inside. At first glance, it was not in too much disarray. All the kitchen cabinets and closet doors were open, but nothing else seemed too disturbed. A bottle of Absolut Citron vodka sat on the kitchen counter, though.

Charles assumed the police had left it there on purpose, knowing he would need a drink when he got home. He filled a glass full of vodka and tossed a few ice cubes in for good measure.

He sat down in the small living area and switched on the television. CNN flashed on the screen. Tired and numb, he stared at the screen without really seeing it. He set his empty glass down on the table next to him and fell asleep.

* * *

THE FOLLOWING MORNING, Charles woke up at 8:00 a.m. He fixed a quick breakfast and decided he needed some fresh air. He walked a block to Klyde Warren Park and then lapped the park five times before returning to his apartment. The walk had the desired effect, and he felt a little more energized.

Charles's cell phone chimed with a reminder to go to Baylor University Medical Center that afternoon to have the sutures in his back removed. With all the recent drama in his life, he had forgotten about the appointment.

After the short trip to the hospital, Charles considered going to his studio to paint. He was hesitant and not sure if Sam would even welcome him back. She might have had enough of all the baggage he had brought to her gallery. Also, it was possible Sam believed he might be guilty of killing that woman or at least...

Charles's phone pinged with a text from Sam.

> Charles, I hope you're doing OK. I went to Lew Sterrett this morning to see if I could pay your bail. BTW, that is something I never thought I would say. Anyway, they told me

you were already released. I wanted to remind you that we have an artist reception on Saturday. As always, you're welcome to have your studio open that evening if you wish.

He texted her back.

Sam, so nice to hear from you. Thank you for attempting to pay my bail. I would love to have my studio open for the event. Most importantly, thank you for not kicking me out. I will be in tomorrow to get my studio ready for Saturday.

Charles' spirits improved for a moment until his thoughts drifted back to the fact someone had tried to kill him, and he was charged with murder.

CHAPTER 24

On Saturday evening, Charles arrived at the gallery at 6:30 to prepare for the opening. When he entered, he spotted Sam on a ladder in the back part of the gallery adjusting the lighting on a painting. She was a perfectionist, even if it meant dangling on a ladder while guests arrived for the opening of an exhibition.

He waved at Sam to get her attention. She smiled at him. "Please come here, Charles. How does the lighting look on this piece?"

"It looks great. Of course, I thought it looked great yesterday before you adjusted the lighting."

"You think I'm a little anal retentive, huh?"

"No, not at all." He winked. "You just have a better eye than I do for these things."

Sam climbed down the ladder. The front door buzzer sounded. Charles said, "Early arrivals."

"Would you mind putting away the ladder while I check on the front?"

"Of course." He wondered if Sam would ask him about his experience in jail.

Charles put the ladder into storage and hurried back to his studio. He switched on the lights and scanned Studio 1. Everything looked ready for visitors if he had any. As was his usual practice, Charles opened a bottle of red wine and a bottle of Chardonnay. He poured himself a glass of Chardonnay, adjusted the volume on his stereo, and sat down in front of his easel.

God, I hope I have some visitors with disposable income come back here!

The artist featured in the gallery's exhibition specialized in Neorealism. Despite it being near the holidays, Sam thought that particular genre of art attracted a healthy crowd of visitors to the gallery opening. Much to Charles's surprise, a steady flow of people made their way back to Studio 1 throughout the course of the evening. Studio 1 had become a known destination for those attending events at the Trinity River Gallery.

Charles was engaged in conversation with a man concerning one of his abstract landscape pieces when across the studio he caught sight of a familiar-looking woman studying one of his paintings. The wheels churned in his head as he tried to place her while continuing the conversation with the man. Charles glanced at the man's empty wine glass and contemplated offering to refill it. However, he was more interested in the woman across the room.

The man decided he had taken up enough of Charles's time and left Studio 1. It was now just the woman and Charles. She turned around from examining another painting and smiled.

A numbing chill shot through Charles's spine like

a bolt of lightning. It was Jamie Simon.

"I'm sorry if I startled you," she said.

"What the hell are *you* doing here?" Charles crossed his arms over his chest.

"Believe it or not, I came to both apologize to you and see your art."

Charles scowled. "*Apologize?*"

"When my attorney informed me that my confession to the police was not allowed to be presented in court, I knew you would have to testify. I gathered from our conversation on the last day of our cruise that you would not voluntarily tell anyone about my confession to you."

After unfolding his arms, Charles took a sip of the remnants of Chardonnay still in his glass. He shook his head and laughed. Jamie had a baffled expression as she stared at him with her ice-blue eyes.

"Excuse me," he said. "I was going to offer you some wine. I was then struck with the irony of offering a glass of wine to the same woman who has attempted to poison me by slipping ketamine into my wine glass."

She grimaced, then smiled. "I see your point. But yes, I would love a glass of Chardonnay."

Charles poured them both a glass. "Would you like to sit down?"

She sat upright on the couch, and Charles reclined in one of his guest chairs. He observed how beautiful Jamie was when she was not under the duress of a trial. She was confident and calm.

"What you mentioned earlier," Charles said, "about me not wanting to testify was correct. One of the detectives on your case threatened to charge me with a misdemeanor if I refused to testify about your confession."

"Really?"

"Yes, he cited a Texas law which requires people to tell the police if they have knowledge a felony has been committed, or something to that effect."

"I see. Well, I'm very sorry you had to testify."

Charles studied her face. "You don't strike me as someone who is very remorseful."

As Jamie took a sip of Chardonnay, her hand trembled. "I can understand why you think that of me. I tried on several occasions to poison you. I feel so contrite about that poor young man at The Adolphus Hotel."

Her ice-blue eyes filled with tears. She set her wine glass on the coffee table and fished a tissue from her purse. She was either sincere or a damn good actress. He was not certain which he believed.

She continued. "I have received a lot of needed therapy. I now completely grasp all the pain I have caused you, the woman at the Nasher Sculpture Center, and that poor young hotel worker."

Charles stretched back in his chair. "If you were truly sorry for your actions, then why didn't you just confess in court what you told me on the cruise?"

"That's *exactly* why I confessed to the police earlier. I was ready to go to prison for my crimes."

"What changed your mind?"

"I did a lot of soul searching. I'm *not* a bad person, Charles. I have a mental illness. The diagnosis is a form of delusional disorder. It's treatable with therapy and medication. After I confessed to the police, my psychiatrist told me I would not be able to get the care I needed in prison. She said I had made such improvement. Then she said something that *really* sunk in."

Jamie paused to take another drink of Chardonnay. Charles remained silent.

She continued. "My psychiatrist said my going to prison would not bring that young man back to life. She told me I could be a productive member of society doing good for others outside of prison. No good would come of me spending the rest of my life behind bars. Despite what she said, I was still resigned to going to prison."

She sniffled and rubbed a knuckle across her upper lip. "When my attorney told me he had prevailed on a motion to throw out my confession because the police had failed to read me my rights, I remembered my psychiatrist's words about being a productive person doing good. That's what I decided to pursue if I wasn't convicted."

Charles hesitated, then said, "Did you tell this psychiatrist that your actions helped contribute to my wife's suicide?"

"Yes, I shared all my personal history with her, including how I lied to your wife."

Sam walked into Studio 1. "Excuse me, am I interrupting anything?"

In a tone ringing with sarcasm, Charles said, "No, Jamie and I were just talking about old times. May I pour you a glass of Cabernet Sauvignon?"

Sam laughed. "That's why I came back here."

While pouring Sam a glass of wine, he said, "Jamie, this is Sam. She owns the gallery."

Sam said, "Pleased to meet you, Jamie."

"Likewise."

Charles handed Sam the glass. "Jamie, would you care for a refill?"

She smiled. "Of course. Thank you." Then she said, "Sam, I love the artist on exhibit in the gallery. She seems to take a slightly different approach to Neorealism. More like Edward Hopper than, say, George Bellows."

Sam raised her eyebrows. "That's an interesting perspective. I haven't really thought of her work in that manner. Now that you mention it, I do see the similarity to Hopper, though."

Charles said, "I didn't know you were into contemporary art, Jamie."

Jamie stared into her glass of Chardonnay. "I developed a taste for it last year. Before long, I was attending events at the Dallas Museum of Art and the Nasher."

Charles smirked. "Yes, I was at those same events. I'm surprised we didn't run into each other."

Mary appeared at the door of Studio 1. "Sam, there's a couple interested in one of the paintings."

Sam said, "Excuse me. Nice to meet you, Jamie."

"Nice to meet you, too." Jamie hesitated, then said to Charles, "I'm not just saying this to flatter you, but I like your figurative work better than the artist on exhibit out there."

Charles gave her a smug grin. "Thank you. I've been more involved in abstract for a while now."

"I noticed you didn't have many images of your figurative work on your website. The ones I did see were already sold."

"You've been to my website? How did you know I was an artist?"

She smiled. "Don't you remember? You testified about it in court."

"That's right. Your attorney drilled me pretty good."

Jamie rolled her eyes. "How does it feel to be on *that* end of cross-examination?"

Charles grimaced. "Well, it's not as much fun as asking the questions."

She pointed to the wall behind Charles. "Tell me about that abstract landscape painting."

He swiveled around to glance over his shoulder, then stood up. "That's a fun piece. It's called *On the Road to Merlot*. That was in a series where I was incorporating wine into my paintings." He walked over to the painting, and she followed him.

He pointed to the middle of the canvas. "See that pinkish hue just above the horizon?"

Jamie leaned in to get a closer look and rested her

hand on Charles's back. "Yes, I see it."

In his mind, Charles flinched, but blamed it on her hand pressing against his brand new scars. "That's actually Merlot wine."

"Really?"

"Yes, it took a lot of trial and error to get wine to be effective as an artistic medium. Wine has to be sealed because it will smear on the canvas if touched. Acrylic is generally sealed with a water-based sealant because it's easier to use. Since wine is water-based, a water-based sealant cannot be used with it."

She removed her hand from his back as she took a step backward. "Then how do you seal it?"

"With an oil-based sealant, which is not permanent. But then I put a water-based sealant on top for a permanent one." Charles laughed and then in a facetious tone said, "Fascinating, right?"

Jamie smiled. "Actually, I find it quite interesting."

Charles noticed her glass of wine was empty. "Care for another?"

"No, that's my limit. I've got to drive back over to Kessler Park."

"Kessler Park is underrated but the most beautiful part of Dallas."

"So you're familiar with the area?" She set her glass down.

"Yes, I'm from Oak Cliff and lived in Kessler Park for many years."

"Well, I'm just renting at the moment and trying to decide what my next step will be." Jamie collected her purse. "Thank you for the wine. It was nice to see you outside of the courtroom."

"Would you like me to walk you to your car? This neighborhood is not the safest place to be at night."

"If it's not too much trouble."

He walked with her to her car, parked nearby, and waited while she opened the door on the driver's side.

"Thank you, Charles. Do you mind if I come back soon to get a closer look at your work?"

"I'm here most afternoons. Or contact me through my website, and I can be here anytime."

She slid into the front seat of her black Lexus UX SUV. Before driving away, she lowered the window a crack. "Good night."

Charles waved and walked the short distance to the gallery. He paused at the door and watched as the taillights of Jamie's car disappeared down Levee Street toward downtown.

She drives a dark colored SUV!

When he opened the door to the gallery, Sam and a young couple emerged from her conference room. Charles walked to the rear of the gallery and sat at the wine bar. Sam and the couple said their good-byes. As soon as they left, Sam locked the door and came to the rear gallery.

"Did you make a sale?" he said.

"Not yet. They want to think about it for a while. Which means I probably won't hear from them again."

He laughed. "Oh, the joys of running an art gallery, right?"

"I'm not certain *joy* is the word I would use to describe what it's like to own a gallery. By the way, Jamie seems like a nice person."

Charles rubbed his hand over his head. "Sometimes appearances can be deceiving."

She frowned. "What do you mean?"

"Do you remember a few months ago when I had to testify at a trial?"

Sam nodded, then took a seat next to him.

"Well, Jamie was the defendant I testified against."

Sam studied Charles's face. "Are you kidding... or wait, you're serious? What did she want?"

"That's the million-dollar question. Jamie wasn't convicted. She said she came in to apologize because I had to testify against her."

"That's crazy, Charles!"

"I know it's crazy. But what's more ludicrous is I think she may be sincere."

Sam rolled her eyes. "Wasn't she the one who tried to poison you because you defended the insurance company that denied her husband's claim for benefits?"

Charles sighed at length. "Yes. My life has become a never-ending David Lynch movie. All these strange characters keep popping up. Hell, I'm even charged with *murder*."

She chuckled. "What's happening with that matter?"

"I'm clueless. I haven't heard anything since I was released from jail. I assume they're still conducting the investigation."

"Well, maybe they'll find the actual murderer."

"God, I hope so! The sooner, the better."

"Shall we call it a night?"

"Sure, let me straighten up my studio, and I'll walk out with you."

When Charles returned to the front of the gallery a few minutes later, Sam stood waiting by the front door. He said, "Do you want to hear the cherry on top for the evening?"

"I'm almost afraid to ask."

"Jamie wants to come back soon and discuss my art in more detail."

Sam laughed. "You have to admit, she does at least pretend to know contemporary art history."

"I wonder if she just Googled *Neorealism* before she came in tonight so she would know some artists' names to throw around."

"You may be right."

Charles said good night to Sam and sat in his car checking email as she drove away from the gallery. He fired up his FIAT Spider and eased it out onto Levee Street. He paused at a stop sign on Levee while he adjusted Pandora to find just the right music to drive the short distance to his apartment.

A car right behind him honked. He would have to pass through three traffic lights on the drive from the Trinity River Gallery to Maple Avenue where he usually made a turn to head toward McKinney Avenue. With almost no traffic that time of night on Oak Lawn Avenue and not in any hurry, Charles drove slower than usual in the right lane. He wondered why the car trailing him didn't go around him in the left lane.

Charles failed to make the first traffic light, and the car remained right behind him. Over the course of a few months, he had learned he would have to hurry to make the second light. Accelerating the Spider, he was able to reach the intersection as the green light turned yellow. The car remained on his tail through the light.

His turn at Maple Avenue was at the final traffic light. It would be close, but he was determined to make the light. It turned yellow as he approached and then red as he entered the intersection to turn right. By the sounds of cars honking, the car behind him ran the light, too. Charles watched in his rearview mirror as the car rounded the turn onto Maple Avenue. As the streetlight lit the car, its shape revealed it to be a black SUV.

What is it with me and dark colored SUVs?

Maple Avenue was a rather shadowy street when it did not intersect another street. Charles could not determine the make and model of the car behind him.

Is that Jamie following me?

The headlights of the car behind him prevented him from identifying the type of SUV. As soon as he reached McKinney Avenue, Charles anticipated ample light. As he approached the intersection, he slowed down on purpose to miss the traffic light. The SUV behind him took a right at the last corner before McKinney Avenue. He could not get a good look at it.

Charles turned right on McKinney Avenue. The usual weekend traffic piled up in the area as he turned into his apartment's driveway. A few cars were ahead of him, waiting to enter the parking garage. Charles kept his eyes glued to the rearview mirror. Several cars passed in opposite directions. He could not be certain if any of them were the SUV that had trailed him.

As soon as Charles exited the elevator on the twelfth floor where his apartment was located, his cell phone chimed, alerting him of an email. He unlocked the door to his apartment and, without flipping on the lights, walked over and sat down in his recliner. The lights from the downtown Dallas buildings filtered in through the window, providing plentiful light. The email was from Jamie.

> Hi, Charles, it was so nice to see you this evening! I loved the whole experience. Whether or not you can bring yourself to fully forgive me, I do sincerely thank you for being a gentleman and listening to me. The wine was heavenly too! :) Your art is absolutely fantastic. I thought about the painting *On the Road to Merlot* on my drive home. It would be perfect in my small living room.

If it is not too inconvenient, could I possibly come by your studio tomorrow afternoon and discuss it? Sleep well, Charles!
Jamie

Charles almost never went into his studio the day after an exhibition opening. He also was not comfortable about being alone in the building with Jamie. This might be a ploy for her to get him alone so she could do him in. Charles questioned whether she had really changed.

Hell, I just testified a few months ago that this woman had confessed to attempting to kill me. There's no way I'm going to let my guard down that easily.

Charles texted her back and said the gallery was closed Sunday and Monday. He suggested perhaps some other afternoon might be better. Jamie responded right away that late Tuesday afternoon would be perfect. He wondered if she was sitting in her Lexus UX SUV texting from his apartment building's driveway, but he was too tired to get up and go over to the window.

CHAPTER 25

Tuesday afternoon, Charles glanced at the clock on his studio wall. It was 4:00 p.m. He decided he was finished painting for the day.

His cell phone chimed. Charles ignored it and instead cleaned his brushes and straightened the paints on his worktable. The buzzer at the gallery's front door sent a faint hum over the music on his stereo. Staring at the canvas on his easel, Charles assessed the day's efforts.

A voice at his studio door said, "Looks like you've been busy."

Charles whipped around in his chair. "Oh, it's you. I didn't hear you come in."

"I'm sorry if I surprised you," Jamie said. She was dressed a dark blue pantsuit and a cream-colored blouse. "I can come back later if I'm disturbing you."

"No, I was just trying to decide where I needed to go next with this painting."

"Did you get my text that I was only a few minutes away from the gallery?"

Charles shook his head. "Sorry, I haven't checked texts in a while. Please come in. Can I offer you a glass of wine?"

"Are *you* having some?" She stepped inside, stiletto heels tapping on the cement floor, and glanced around.

"Of course." He winked at her. "It's bad luck to discuss art unless done over a glass of wine."

Jamie smiled. "In that case, I will *definitely* have a glass of white wine, then."

"Sonoma-Cutrer Chardonnay okay for you?"

"Excellent." She set her brown leather purse on the coffee table.

Charles poured two glasses. "I moved the painting we discussed over there where the lighting is perfect." He pointed toward the far wall.

Jamie walked over to the painting and studied it. "I really *love* this painting. I positively want to buy it."

He took a swig. "Sounds good to me. Would you like me to wrap it up for the ride home?"

"Thank you, but that won't be necessary. I can lay it flat in the trunk of my SUV. It should be fine." She took a sip of her Chardonnay. "As I recall from your website, the painting is three thousand dollars."

"That's the list price. You get my thirty percent discount for friends. Let's round the discount up one hundred dollars, so the price for you is two thousand dollars."

"Oh, Charles, are you sure?" she gushed, holding her clasped hands to her chest.

"Most definitely." He grinned. "There're two conditions, though."

Jamie laughed. "Conditions? I'm almost afraid to

ask what those conditions could be."

Charles was a little concerned his cynical sense of humor might not be well received. Nevertheless, he decided to go for it. "The *first* condition is that you don't attempt to kill me anymore." He paused to see how Jamie would respond.

With a twinkle in her eye, she laughed as she stared at him and said, "And the second condition?"

"You will have dinner with me some night."

Jamie took another sip. "You got a deal. I have one condition as well."

"What's that?"

She tilted her head to one side and gave him a sly grin. "My condition is that you promise *not* to wait too long before you take me to dinner."

"Agreed."

Mary handled the sale of the painting, and Charles carried it out to Jamie's car. He stood on the sidewalk in front of the gallery and watched as she drove away.

Why the hell did I ask her to dinner? Do I have a death wish or am I simply a complete idiot?

CHAPTER 26

Charles waited several days before he reached out to Jamie. He sent her an email asking how the painting looked in her living room. She responded that it was a perfect fit and sent him an image of the painting positioned over her sofa.

Charles found it very strange to be both attracted to and afraid of someone, but that is the exact predicament he faced. He never blamed Jamie for his wife's suicide; rather he forced himself to admit that his inexcusable behavior, over many years of a detached relationship, caused his wife's decision.

While mulling it over for a few more days, Charles had grown even more uncertain about setting a date for dinner with Jamie. Perhaps she sensed his reluctance or was just toying with him, because she called Charles.

"Hello."

Jamie's tone was abrupt. "Well, are we *still* on for dinner?"

Attempting not to resemble an awkward teenage boy, he muttered, "I was just getting ready to call you. Are you free next Tuesday night?"

"I'm just playing with you," Jamie said as she laughed. "You don't have to ask me to dinner if you are hesitant."

"Oh no, I'm not the least bit hesitant. Is Tuesday convenient?"

Jamie paused as if to check the calendar on her iPhone. "Yes, I'm free this coming Tuesday. What did you have in mind?"

"How about Fearing's?" *That place should be plenty crowded if she tries something.*

"Sounds good. I was just thinking about Fearing's the other night as I drove in the uptown area. I haven't been there in years."

"Would you like me to pick you up," Charles said, "or would you prefer to meet me there?" He ran a hand over his bald head and hoped for the answer he preferred.

"Let's just meet in the lobby of The Ritz-Carlton. Besides, didn't you tell me that you lived in the area?"

As he heaved a sigh of relief, Charles could not remember telling Jamie where he lived. "Yes, my apartment is just a few blocks from the hotel. I'll make reservations for 7:30 p.m. Shall we meet around 7:00 and have a cocktail in the bar before dinner?"

"Perfect! I'm looking forward to it."

Before ending the phone call, he said, "By the way, thank you again for purchasing one of my paintings."

"I love it. Thank you, Charles."

"Goodbye, Jamie."

"Goodbye."

Charles tossed his phone on his kitchen counter. *I can't believe I have a date with the woman who tried to kill me not once, but several times.*

He closed his eyes and rubbed his temples. *I'm curious as hell to see if she's truly reformed. The evening could be a real Hitchcock experience!*

He opened his eyes. *How can I resist?*

CHAPTER 27

At 6:00 p.m. Tuesday, Charles stood in front of a mirror trying to decide what to wear on a date with a confessed murderer. Should he go casual or dress up for the occasion?

He opted to dress up and put on his charcoal-gray suit, light-blue shirt, and no tie. He had donated all but one of his suits to charity after retiring from his law practice.

It was a cool, crisp, December night. At 6:45 p.m., Charles exited his apartment building and walked the short stretch of McKinney Avenue north to where The Ritz-Carlton was located. The covered driveway in front of the hotel was full of expensive cars, most of them Mercedes and Jaguars, waiting to be parked.

A doorman opened the front door for Charles. As he made his way to the middle of the lobby, he scanned the room, looking for Jamie. She was nowhere in sight. He wanted a stiff cocktail to calm his nerves but instead found a chair outside of the Rattlesnake Bar, where he could still listen to the piano music in the bar piped from the speakers in the ornate ceiling.

After a few minutes, Charles spotted Jamie entering the lobby. He rose to his feet and waved. As she walked toward him, Charles pondered if he should initiate a hug or just stand his ground.

She pointed first to her dark-gray pantsuit, then to his. "You and I look like twins."

He smiled. "I only have one suit, so my choice for the evening was charcoal gray or charcoal gray."

"Hope I didn't keep you waiting long."

"Not at all. Would you still care to have a quick drink before we go to dinner?"

"Sure."

He motioned in the direction of the bar and followed Jamie inside. They both perched on dark leather barstools at the end of the bar, away from the other well-dressed customers.

The bartender approached and said, "May I help you?"

Jamie said, "I think I'll have a glass of Chardonnay."

The bartender looked at Charles.

"I'll have an Absolut Citron vodka and soda."

The bartender returned with their order and placed their drinks in front of them. Charles picked up his cocktail and tilted it toward her. "Cheers."

"Cheers." Their glasses clinked together. "Here's to great art."

"I like that."

She set her drink down and shifted in her seat toward him. "May I ask you a question, Charles?"

"Sure."

"Were you apprehensive about going to dinner with me?"

"Truthfully?" He stared at her reflection in the bar mirror, then turned toward her. "Yes."

"Why did you ask me, then?"

"I'm not sure I can articulate why. Perhaps I wanted to experience the surreal absurdity of having dinner with someone who previously had tried to murder me."

Jamie took a sip of wine. "How's this surreal absurdity of a dinner date turning out for you?"

Charles laughed. "I'm sitting in this bar with a beautiful woman having a predinner drink. So it must be going okay."

She looked at her iPhone. "It's almost 7:30 p.m. Should we check in with the hostess?"

They were seated at a corner table in the main dining room. Charles always used to request this spot over the more boisterous dining area with a view of the kitchen. Charles and Jamie enjoyed a lovely meal accompanied by a Ramey Chardonnay, a perfect pairing.

"Will you excuse me just a second," Charles said, "while I step into the restroom?"

"You're not going to run off and leave me with the bill, are you?" said Jamie with a smirk.

"No, I'll definitely be back."

When Charles returned to the table, Jamie's purse was sitting on the table next to his wine glass. The scene was identical to one on the cruise when she had set her purse on the table and pretended to pour poison into his wine.

He stared at his glass. It was about one-third full. Charles could not remember how much had remained in his glass when he had excused himself. He was hesitant to drink any more.

The waiter poured the last remnants of wine from the bottle into Jamie's glass.

"It just occurred to me," Charles said, "that we have something very unusual in common."

Jamie twirled her glass of wine. "Really? What might that be?"

"Well, in keeping with the surreal theme of the evening, we both have been accused of murder."

Eyes narrowed, she studied Charles's face. "What do you mean?"

"You've been accused of murder and in fact even tried in court. I haven't been formally indicted, but I was accused of murdering some poor woman in Reverchon Park."

"W-w-what ha-happened?"

"I was hiking in the park one morning and met a woman out walking her dog. We briefly engaged in conversation, and I petted her dog. Later that same morning, she was murdered near where we had met. My business card was found a few feet from the body. The police matched my fingerprints to the prints taken from the dog's collar. Then they made the quantum leap from there to accusing me of murder."

Jamie's eyebrows shot up. "They found your business card near the body?"

Charles twisted his mouth into a wry smile. "Yes,

my card has had a bad habit over the past few months of showing up at various crime scenes."

"Are you serious?" She patted his forearm.

"Yes, as ridiculous as it sounds, someone has been leaving my card behind to try and convince the police that I committed these crimes."

"That's ridiculous. I can't believe the cops would even imagine you are so stupid as to leave your card at a crime scene."

"Believe it or not, one of the detectives investigating the murder theorizes that it's a clever ruse on my part to outwit the police." Charles stared at the last bit of Chardonnay in his glass, lifted it to his lips, then set it down right away.

Jamie finished off her final sip of wine. "Well, this certainly has been an interesting evening."

"I apologize for making that comparison. About what you and I have in common, I mean." He winced. "Sometimes my attempt at humor is ill-conceived."

"No need to apologize, Charles. After all, you wanted a surreal date for the evening. Mission accomplished."

He signaled the waiter for his check.

"Aren't you going to finish your glass?" Jamie said. "The wine was exquisite."

Charles smirked. "No, I think I've had enough."

He paid the check, and they exited the dining room into the lobby of the hotel.

"Did you walk here?" said Jamie.

"Yes, I live only a few blocks south down the

street." He pointed in that direction.

"Can I give you a lift back to your apartment?"

"No, but I appreciate your offer. I believe I'll walk home to get a bit of exercise."

Jamie said, "Well. Thank you for dinner." She turned and strolled toward the front door, leaving Charles standing alone in the lobby.

Charles waited several minutes without moving. He wanted to make sure Jamie was already gone before he left. As he exited the hotel, he heaved a long exhale when she was nowhere in sight.

Instead of walking straight home south on McKinney Avenue, Charles crossed the street and headed over to Klyde Warren Park. Feeling comfortable since it was still crowded with people at this hour, he lapped the park and then walked the short block back to his apartment. He scanned his fob to open the front door to his apartment building.

The woman working the concierge desk said, "Good evening, Mr. Pierce."

"Good evening."

"Jason, one of our night valets," she said, "asked me to let you know that this envelope with your name on it was found resting on the valet stand."

"Oh, thanks." Charles took the envelope and rode the elevator up to the twelfth floor. As soon as he was inside his apartment, he ripped open the envelope. Inside was a printed note that warned, *Stay away from Levee Street. I won't miss next time.*

A single bullet dropped out of the envelope, fell

onto the kitchen counter, and rolled to a stop next to his toaster.

What the hell?

Pacing in the kitchen, he called the concierge desk. "Hello, this is Charles Pierce in 1206. Would it be possible for me to speak to the valet who found the envelope addressed to me?"

The woman at the desk said, "Would you like me to send him to your apartment?"

"Yes, if you could, please. I won't take too much of his time." He stood still at the counter, trying not to shake from the knees up.

Ten minutes later, a knock came at his door. When he opened it, a young man stood there in his valet uniform.

Charles said, "Please come in..." He double-checked the valet's name tag. "...Jason."

"Yes, sir."

"I understand you were the one who found the envelope addressed to me?" He picked it up from the counter and turned it to face the valet.

"Yes, sir. It was sitting on top of the valet stand when I returned from parking a car."

Charles set the envelope down. "Did you see anyone who might have placed it there?"

"No, sir. I was parking Mr. Johnson's car and found it when I returned."

"I take it Mr. Johnson is a resident here."

"Yes, sir."

"I thought you just parked the cars of visitors to

the apartment." He arched one eyebrow.

"That's usually the case."

Charles stared at the valet as if inspecting his skin for wrinkles. "Why do you suppose Mr. Johnson didn't just park himself?"

"He had just returned from the grocery store and his car was full of groceries. I got him the cart so he could haul them up to his apartment. He asked if I wouldn't mind parking his car for him."

"I see. Was there anyone else hanging around the area?"

The valet shrugged. "There's always people coming and going."

Charles couldn't think of any further questions. "Okay, thank you for coming up. I'm sorry I pestered you with all these inquiries."

"No problem, Mr. Pierce."

The young man let himself out of the apartment. Charles proceeded to read and reread the note.

Why does someone want me to stay away from the Trinity River Gallery? He set the sheet of paper on the counter. *Much as I hate to do it, I'm going to call Detective Gonzales tomorrow.*

He then recalled in horror that where he and Jamie were seated in the restaurant had always been his late wife's favorite spot.

The hits just keep on coming.

CHAPTER 28

The next morning, Charles called Detective Gonzales and told him about the envelope. The detective said he would stop by Charles's studio at around 4:00 p.m.

Charles arrived at the gallery at 3:30 p.m. He debated whether or not he should tell Sam about the threat he had received. Only Mary was at the gallery. She informed him Sam was running errands.

Charles waited in his studio for Detective Gonzales to arrive. Promptly at 4:00 p.m., the front door of the gallery buzzed. After about five minutes, the detective made his way back to Studio 1. He walked through the open door. "Hello, Pierce."

"Good afternoon, Detective."

Charles had placed the envelope, note, and bullet on his coffee table. Detective Gonzales hovered over the three items but was careful not to touch them. "Care to flip the envelope over so I can see the side with your name on it?"

Charles did as the detective requested. "There's no return address, if that's what you were checking."

The detective leaned over it, then backed up a bit to get rid of his shadow from the overhead light fixture. "No, I just wanted to make sure I saw both sides. It appears to be the same text as used on the note. Just the one bullet inside, correct?"

"Yes. It fell onto my kitchen counter when I pulled the note out."

The detective studied it at close range. "That's a .357 Magnum. Very interesting."

"Interesting in what way?"

"It's a different kind of bullet than the one we dug out of the gallery wall."

"What kind was the one in the wall?"

"A nine-millimeter."

Palms forward, Charles shrugged. "Why's that significant?"

Detective Gonzales plopped down in one of the client chairs and frowned right away. "I forgot how damn uncomfortable your chairs are in here." He fidgeted for a moment, then said, "Forensics said the gallery shot came from a German-manufactured pistol. They're not commonly found in the United States. If the same person is involved, why would he shoot at you with one type of bullet and leave a note with a different type? In other words, wouldn't he leave you a threatening note with the type of bullet he in fact fired from his pistol?"

Charles sat down across from him. "Really, they can pinpoint the type of pistol used?"

"Not always, but in some cases they can."

"What happens next, Detective?"

"I will put the envelope, note, and bullet in an evidence bag and assign it a case file. There's not much else that can be done."

Detective Gonzales pulled some plastic gloves and a clear, plastic evidence bag from his coat pocket. Charles watched as he sealed the items in the bag and removed his gloves.

"What about the Reverchon Park case?" Charles said. "Any new developments there?"

"Possibly. A man and his dog were in the park yesterday and came across a pipe wrench. This man fancies himself an amateur sleuth. He read about the woman's body found in the park and went there to conduct his own investigation. He alerted the police and was careful not to touch or otherwise disturb the wrench. Even if it turns out to be the weapon, someone else might have previously stumbled upon it earlier and tampered with it."

Charles sat up straight and clapped his hands. "That's encouraging, Detective! Has forensics examined it yet?"

Detective Gonzales shook his head. "Not yet. It takes a while."

"I'm surprised I haven't heard anything from the court about the case."

"That's because nothing has been presented to the grand jury yet. The prosecutors are dragging their feet. They're probably hoping more evidence surfaces."

Charles snorted. "I suspected something like that was happening. Maybe the DA knows they would have trouble convicting me just because I petted that poor woman's dog. Nothing else ties me to the crime. I haven't even hired an attorney yet to represent me."

Detective Gonzales leaned forward. "You better hope the pipe wrench doesn't have your DNA on it."

Charles scowled at him. "You don't really believe I murdered that woman, do you?"

"It doesn't matter what I think. All that matters is what the grand jury thinks when the DA presents the case to them." Detective Gonzales stood up. "Okay, Pierce, I'm out of here. Try not to get your ass shot."

"I'll do my best," he said with a chuckle.

After Detective Gonzales left, Charles was lost in mental scenarios. He vacillated between being target practice for someone with a German pistol and the pipe wrench found at Reverchon Park.

"Good afternoon, Charles." Sam stood at the entrance of the studio.

He jolted upright. "Oh, hey, Sam. How's it going?"

"Since it's almost 5:00 p.m.," she said as she sauntered into the room, "I was wondering why you haven't offered me a glass of wine yet."

He glanced at his wall clock. "I was just going to come up front and do that very thing. How about a glass of Zinfandel?"

"Sounds wonderful."

He poured a glass for each of them. "How's your day going?"

"Uneventful. I've spent almost the *entire* day packing art and shipping it to back to an artist in

Brazil. I'm not sure it's worth representing inter-national talent. Just a lot of work and hassle. How about you?"

Charles took a sip of wine. "I spent some qual-ity time this afternoon with my good friend Detective Gonzales."

"I saw him when he left the gallery. What did he want?"

"I contacted him about a very mysterious package I received last evening at my apartment. Someone left an envelope with my name on it at the valet stand. The guy working valet that night didn't see who left it."

"A mysterious package?"

"Yes, it contained a note warning me to stay away from Levee Street and assuring me they won't miss next time. Included was a single bullet, which I guess was for emphasis."

Frowning, Sam took a drink of wine. "That's very bizarre. Who would leave you that type of note?"

"I'm clueless."

"What did the detective say?"

"He took it as evidence," Charles said with a shrug, "but indicated there was not much more the police could do at this point."

"Charles, do you think it was that same guy who threatened you at our exhibition opening?"

He set his wine glass down. "That's definitely crossed my mind. But how would he know where I lived?"

"Maybe he followed you home from the gallery some night."

"Well, I've had the feeling I've been followed on more than one occasion by a black SUV."

"Really? The same car every time?"

Charles leaned back in his chair. "I can't be certain. It might have been."

Sam finished her glass of wine. "What kind of bullet was in the envelope?"

"I don't know anything about guns. The detective, though, said it was .357 Magnum."

"Hang on just a second. I'll be right back."

She returned five minutes later with her pistol. "This is a Smith & Wesson nine-millimeter. It's a great pistol for target practice." Sam pointed it at one of Charles's paintings.

"Be careful with that. I like that painting."

"Don't worry, Charles, it's not loaded." She continued. "Simone inherited a P38 nine-millimeter Luger from her dad. It's a relic, but it's still pretty cool as well."

Charles smiled. "I'll take your word for it." He thought about the bullet lodged in the gallery wall. "Does Simone's gun fire a .357 Magnum?"

"No, it fires a nine-millimeter, like mine. Why? Do you think *Simone* is the culprit who left you the threatening note?"

He pursed his lips during a moment of reflection, then said, "Would you like a refill?"

"No, I need to do a few things before I call it quits

for the evening."

Charles refilled his glass. "I don't know who left me the note. However, since a black SUV has been following me and we know Simone drives that type of car... So I'm just saying it's a possibility she might be that person."

Sam frowned. "Simone can be a little unhinged at times. However, I could never see her doing something so extreme and dangerous."

"You're probably right. I know I'm just clutching at straws. On the other hand, it could be Jamie."

"What makes you think that?" She tucked the pistol under her arm.

"When she purchased one of my paintings, I carried it out to her car. She drives a black Lexus SUV."

"Don't you guess she's a better suspect than Simone? After all, she's already tried to kill you on several occasions."

"You make a persuasive argument." He gave a reluctant nod. "By the way, you're not going to believe my next bit of news."

Sam's expression revealed a cross between bewilderment and curiosity. "Why won't I believe it?"

"You may want another glass of wine."

She laughed. "All right, pour me another glass."

Charles filled her glass with Zinfandel and took a swig of his wine. "I had dinner at Fearing's with Jamie last night."

Sam's mouth dropped open. "First, you sell a painting to someone who tried to kill you, and then you turn around and have a *dinner date* with her?"

Charles groaned. "Yes, that's correct."

"How in the world did that come about?"

"I gave her a discount on the price of the painting conditioned upon her going to dinner with me."

"Are you insane? Why on earth would you do something like that?"

Charles smiled. "I told Jamie I asked her out for the surreal absurdity of going on a date with someone who had previously tried to murder me."

Sam rolled her eyes. "How did she react to that reason?"

"About like you would've expected."

"I can only imagine your dinner conversation." She smirked and shook her head.

"It was actually fairly normal and enjoyable until the end."

"What happened at the end?"

"I told Jamie she and I had something unusual in common."

"I'm almost afraid to ask what that is." She put her hand to her mouth.

Charles grinned. "I told her we both had been charged with murder."

Sam rolled her eyes again. "I can understand how that comparison would not be well received."

"Let's just say we got our check and parted ways. She was kind enough to offer me a lift back to my apartment, though. I declined and decided to get some exercise. I went over to Klyde Warren Park for a while before returning to my apartment. When I walked in my building, the concierge handed me the envelope containing the note and bullet. She said it was left on the valet stand."

"Do you think it's possible Jamie drove to your apartment and left the envelope before you had a chance to get back there?"

"Hmmmm." Charles frowned. "Yes, there was definitely time. But if she had planned on doing that, then why would she offer to drive me home?"

"I don't know. I guess she could have left the envelope on the valet stand after you got out of her car and entered your apartment building."

"Yeah, well, that's a possibility."

Sam took a drink. "Did you tell the detective about your dinner date?"

"Hell no! Detective Gonzales would've accused me of conspiring with Jamie when I testified against her in court. He was desperate to get her convicted since they botched the Miranda warning and couldn't use her confession against her. I was supposed to be the prosecutor's star witness. My testimony of her confession would have almost guaranteed her conviction."

Sam checked the time on the studio wall clock. "It's been interesting, Charles. Nevertheless, I have to run."

After Charles locked the door to his studio, he exited through the front door and drove home from the gallery. The traffic was light on Oak Lawn Avenue. By habit now, he checked his rearview mirror and heaved a sigh when no one appeared to be following him. If someone was, he or she was damn good, because the traffic flow looked normal.

He pulled into his parking place and caught the elevator up to the twelfth floor. Charles entered his apartment, poured a glass of wine, and sat down at the computer. He just remembered he had failed to tell Sam about the police's identification of the type of bullet lodged in the gallery wall.

Sam said Simone's gun was a nine-millimeter. She referred to it as a relic and that Simone had inherited a Luger.

Charles typed Luger pistol into a web browser. He hit the Wikipedia link and read:

> The Pistole Parabellum—or Parabellum-Pistole (Pistol Parabellum), commonly known as just Luger[7]—is a toggle-locked recoil-operated semi-automatic pistol that was produced in several models and by several nations from 1898 to 1948.
>
> The design was first patented by Georg Luger as an improvement upon the Borchardt Automatic Pistol and was produced as the Parabellum Automatic Pistol, Borchardt-Luger System by the German arms manufacturer Deutsche Waffen und Munitionsfabriken (DWM).[1]

German arms manufacturer! Charles leaned back

in his chair and blinked twice. *Detective Gonzales said forensics identified the bullet in the gallery as a nine-millimeter fired from a German pistol.*

He was convinced that Simone was the individual who had both shot at him and left him the note.

But what do I do with this information? Yikes, what if I'm wrong?

He pulled up the Dallas County Appraisal District's website on his computer. He did not know Simone's last name, so he typed in Samantha Sterling. It took a while to scroll through all the Sterlings in Dallas County, but he soon located a property belonging to Samantha Sterling and Simone Altmann, 627 Diceman Drive.

Now that he had the information he needed, Charles planned to do a little investigation of his own into Simone.

CHAPTER 29

The next afternoon, it was time to lease a car to be more incognito. If Simone had been the one following him, his FIAT Spider would be instantly recognizable. Living within walking distance of downtown Dallas had its perks, since several rental car companies were located near his apartment.

Charles chose a black Buick Encore from Enterprise Rent-A-Car. He walked the short distance and picked up his vehicle. Now that he had the address and the rental car, he had to determine his plan of action. His initial step would be to get the license plate number on Simone's SUV. Charles had attempted to find it online, but privacy laws had prevented it.

At 8:00 p.m., Charles typed in Simone and Sam's address into his navigator app and took off to his destination. It took him thirty minutes to reach their neighborhood. As he rounded the corner onto Diceman Drive, he slowed to 10 mph past their house, a small, wood-and-brick, cottage-type house built in the 1940s. No lights were on, nor was there a car in the driveway.

He drove around the block and then parked one house down in front of a vacant lot across the street to wait, in case Simone came home. The neighborhood was situated near White Rock Lake, where builders were razing many of the smaller houses to allow for much larger new homes. Charles hoped he was not acting too conspicuous. He questioned why he had thought it was beneficial to stake out the house just to find out Simone's license plate number.

After ten more minutes, Charles started his car, and headlights reflected in his rearview mirror. He covered his face, pretending to be on the phone as the car drove past him and pulled into the driveway.

My God, that's Sam's car! He gripped the steering wheel tighter. *She told me she had moved out. What the hell is she doing here?*

Charles watched as Sam unlocked the front door and entered the house. Room by room the lights in the house turned on. He shifted the Buick into drive and eased past the house, around the corner, and then back west toward downtown. He had done enough sleuthing for the night.

* * *

THE NEXT MORNING, Charles deliberated whether to turn the rental car in and give up his investigation of Simone. But if he drove by the house one more time, what was there to lose?

Charles turned the corner onto Diceman Drive and parked in the same location as last night. No cars were parked in the house's driveway. He noticed, though, the garage door had two small windows on the right and left side.

Should I check if I can see Simone's license plate from one of the windows? He bit his lip. *What if I get caught?*

Charles exited the Buick and walked down the sidewalk across from the house. He crossed the street in front of the house and spotted an advertisement newspaper lying on the grass next to the driveway. He picked up the newspaper and headed up the driveway. If one of the neighbors saw him, they would reason he was just being neighborly by putting the misdirected newspaper on the porch.

He had no excuse if Simone spotted him. He decided it was worth the risk.

Charles sauntered up the driveway and paused to look through one of the windows in the garage. But she had backed into the garage and the front of her car had no license plates. Although Texas law mandated that all vehicles have front license plates, the police almost never enforced the law. As a result, many people opted not to install the front license plates.

Simone's next-door neighbor opened her front door, and a German shepherd bounded out the door and off the porch in Charles's direction. Charles gasped and held his breath.

The neighbor shouted, "Freeze, Jaxx!"

Charles exhaled when the dog obeyed his owner. Jaxx sat staring at Charles.

"Can I help you with something?" The neighbor's tone reeked with suspicion.

He turned to face her. "No, I'm a friend of Simone and Sam."

"Why were you looking into their garage window?"

"I... I w-was in the n-n-neighborhood and... thought I would stop... stop by for a visit. I looked into the garage window to ... to see if anyone was home. There are no cars, so I guess they're not here." He gambled the neighbor would not peer through the same window and discover he was lying. He could not tell her Simone's car was in the garage. Otherwise, she would expect him to ring the doorbell, and that was something he had to avoid.

"Shall I tell them you stopped by?" the neighbor said.

Charles shook his head. "No, thank you. I'll give them a call later on."

He tossed the newspaper onto the porch and waved at the neighbor as he hurried back to his car. The neighbor and Jaxx were still watching as he drove away.

That's it! I'm done investigating!

* * *

WHILE DRIVING TO the gallery that afternoon, Charles wondered if he should tell Sam about the type of bullet found in the gallery wall. He was uncertain of the appropriate course of action. When he arrived, the front door buzzed as he entered. Mary emerged from the back of the building. "Hello, Charles."

"Hey, Mary. How's it going?"

"Fine, and you?"

"Okay. Is Sam here?"

"No, she's out running errands. By the way, a woman came by earlier asking to see you."

"Really? Did she say what she wanted?"

Mary ran her hand through her hair. "No. She said she hadn't seen you in a while and heard you had a studio here."

"Well, that's interesting. Did she give you her name?"

"No. Sorry, Charles, I probably should have asked her."

"What did she look like?"

Mary again got that perplexed expression when she was asked to describe what someone looked like. "Tall, thin, dark-haired, and attractive."

Charles feigned anger. "Damn it, why didn't you get her name and phone number?" He winked at her.

"It's more fun this way." Mary smiled. "Now you'll be surprised when she returns."

"What if she doesn't ever come back? Then I'll never know."

"Well, then you'll just have to use your imagination."

"All right, you win."

She smiled again. "You give up too easily."

Charles laughed. "Time for me to go paint. Wine

at 4:30 p.m. if you have an interest."

After over two hours of painting, the front door of the gallery buzzed. Charles guessed it must be Sam returning from running her errands.

Someone walked in the hallway outside of his studio. When the footsteps stopped, Charles set his brush down.

Rounding the corner, he spotted Rachel Holbrook, the manager of The Wine Therapist, viewing one of his paintings. Charles was a regular patron of The Wine Therapist when he lived in the heart of downtown. He had spent many afternoons perched on the end stool at the bar, imbibing on whatever Chardonnay was featured.

"Hey, beautiful!" he called. "What brings you to this neck of the woods?"

She laughed. "I wanted to see what my favorite artist and former best patron was up to these days."

"As you can see, I no longer maintain my studio in my cramped apartment."

Rachel drew closer to Charles, and they embraced, a ritual they used to practice every time he entered The Wine Therapist. She was a nice, supporting soul who gave true meaning to the therapist part of the name for many of the bar's usual crowd.

Charles said, "My God, I've missed you."

"Whose fault is *that*? I'm still managing the bar, but you've been missing in action since you moved to that swanky, palatial apartment uptown."

"That's true. The only thing swanky and palatial is

the view. I have the smallest apartment in the entire building." He waved toward the door to his studio. "Anyway, please come in and make yourself at home. I need to clean my brushes before the acrylic dries."

Rachel circled Studio 1 taking in the art while Charles left to go clean his brushes. Upon returning, he glanced at his wall clock. It was 3:30 p.m. "I know it's a tad early, but may I offer you a glass of Frank Family Cabernet?"

"Excellent wine!" She grinned. "How can I refuse?"

Charles opened a bottle and filled her glass almost to the rim. "I'm just trying to emulate my favorite wine bar manager's generosity." Then he poured himself a glass of Chardonnay.

Rachel said, "Cheers."

"Cheers." He held up his glass and tilted it toward her. "So Rachel, how did you know my studio was down here?"

She took a swig. "Your website. By the way, this is a lovely wine."

Charles smiled. "You checked my website and just had to come see for yourself if it was accurate?"

"Actually, I have an ulterior motive."

"Really?" He smirked at her. "What could that be?"

"You know we exhibit artists at The Wine Therapist. I wanted to see if you'd agree to display some of your art there."

"People don't come to The Wine Therapist to see art. They come in to drink wine, see you, or both. Has an artist *ever* sold any piece on exhibit there?"

She smiled. "Believe it or not, they do on occasion."

Charles took a drink of Chardonnay. He doubted any patron had ever bought a painting exhibited in The Wine Therapist. "May I think about it?"

"Don't think too long. I need someone yesterday. The artist who was supposed to exhibit flaked out on me. I hate staring at bare walls."

"Artists are creative sorts but not always reliable." He paused. "All right, how many pieces would you like me to hang?"

"Enough to fill up the north wall. Besides, it will be like old times. We can catch up on things."

Charles set his wine glass down on the coffee table. "Okay, I'll do it.

"Thank you," she gushed. "What's been going on? Have you been staying out of trouble?"

"Hardly. Over the course of the last month, I've been shot at and arrested for homicide."

As her mouth dropped open, Rachel raised her eyebrows. "What? You're not serious."

"I'm afraid I'm very much so! They're both long stories. Obviously, I didn't kill anyone. At least, I hope that's obvious. However, I had the misfortune of petting the victim's dog before its owner was murdered. My fingerprints were found on the dog's collar. That's the only thing that tied me to the victim. Well, that and the fact the police also found my business card nearby. I know what you're going to ask. Somebody has been planting my business cards at various crime scenes. I've no clue as to why."

Rachel took a large swig of wine. "Well, that's the homicide part. What about the getting-shot-at part?"

"I think, but I'm not one hundred percent certain, the two events are unrelated. It happened here one night when I was leaving the gallery. Before I could get to my car, someone fired two shots at me. One of them shattered the front window of the gallery. I still have scars on my back from the shards of glass that rained down on me."

She gasped. "That's horrifying, Charles!"

"Believe it or not, it gets even more unreal. Do you remember the woman who was stalking and trying to poison me last year?"

"Yes, I remember. She even came in The Wine Therapist a few times."

"Well, guess what? I had a dinner date with her."

Rachel's mouth dropped open again. "You have to be joking now."

"Nope," he said with a slight shrug, followed by a grin. "She even bought a painting from me."

"Charles, you're hopeless."

"Maybe hopeless, but never boring. Are you sure you want me to hang some art at The Wine Therapist? There's no telling what catastrophes will descend upon the bar."

Rachel laughed. "I'm willing to risk it. Can you come tomorrow around 3:00 p.m.?"

"I'll be there."

"Got to run. Please be careful."

They hugged, and Charles walked with her through the gallery to the front. "Are you parked close by?"

"That's my little Hyundai right there." She pointed out the front window at a yellow coupe.

"Great. See you tomorrow."

"Bye, Charles."

When he turned around, Sam was standing in the doorway of her office. "A potential art collector or love interest?" Her toned dripped with facetiousness.

Charles smiled. "Neither. Rachel manages a wine bar called The Wine Therapist. Before I moved, I was a regular there. She asked if I would hang some of my art there. Apparently, an artist she had lined up for an exhibit flaked on her."

"I see." She paused. "And I can see you were also enjoying some wine." Sam gestured toward his right hand.

Charles gave a slight jerk as he glanced down. He was still carrying his wine glass. "Yes, I am. Would you care for some?"

"Sure, I'll be back there in about ten minutes. I also need to ask you a huge favor."

"Sounds intriguing."

Charles went back to his studio and poured himself another glass of Chardonnay. As promised, Sam walked into his gallery a few minutes later. He poured her a glass of the same Cabernet Sauvignon he had served Rachel.

"Ah, very nice aroma." Sam swirled the wine in

her glass, then took a sip. "Excellent taste."

"I love all the Frank Family wines."

They both sat down in Charles's guest chairs. "So what's this huge favor you need to ask of me?"

"Simone needs to have some surgery and will be laid up for some time. Someone will have to take care of her for a couple of weeks. She's estranged from everyone in her family except her dad, and he's incapacitated. Simone was desperate, so she called, and I dropped by last night."

Maybe Sam had spotted him sitting across the street from the house in his rental car. He said, "It's nice you're both still on good terms."

She nodded, her head bobbing like a fishing float. "In an emergency, you do what you need to do. I would hope she would do the same for me if ever needed."

Charles took a drink. "Where do I fit into all of this?"

"I have a Pop Art exhibition on the calendar in three weeks. I have done some of the legwork, but there's still much to be done. Will you take over for me and curate the exhibition?"

Charles rubbed his chin. "Is Mary not capable of curating it?"

"Mary doesn't have any experience. I'll need her to do some of the more mundane tasks like shipping artwork and greeting guests."

"You do realize, Sam, I don't have any experience either?" He arched one eyebrow. "I'll be flying by the seat of my pants."

Sam smiled. "According to your website, you have exhibited in several galleries across North America."

Charles shook his head. "Participating as an artist is much different than curating an exhibit."

"I know, but you've got more practical knowledge than Mary. You will do just fine."

"What's left to be done in preparation?"

She took a drink. "First, we need about three more artists. Each will be given space for three paintings, depending upon their size. Second, I need you to promote it in the media. I'll email you the list of media contacts. Last, I'll need you to hang the art and adjust the lighting."

"What about wine and any food?"

"Mary can handle those details."

"Will you be able to attend the opening night?"

"Yes, unless Simone has some kind of setback."

He sat in silence for a moment. "All right, Sam, I'll do it."

She stood, walked over, and hugged Charles. "Thank you so much."

"What's the name for the exhibition?"

Sam laughed. "That's up to the curator."

He gave a low whistle. "Nothing like putting a little pressure on the resident artist. I'll get started tonight."

Sam stared down at their empty wine glasses sitting on the coffee table. "I need to do a few more things in my office before I leave. Would you like me to take these glasses to the kitchen?"

"No, thanks, I'll get them. Please remember to send me the media contact information."

"Will do. Thanks again, Charles." Sam exited Studio 1.

Holy cow, what did I get myself into this time?

Before leaving, Charles straightened up his studio. On his way to the front of the gallery, he considered telling Sam that police forensics had determined the bullet lodged in the gallery wall was from a German pistol. He felt desperate to see her reaction, but he decided the timing was not right.

Besides, if his suspicions were correct that Simone was the culprit, she would not be in any condition to cause him any harm for a while. Instead, he would laser focus on making the upcoming exhibition a success.

What could possibly go wrong?

CHAPTER 30

Charles spent the better part of the evening researching artists who specialized in Pop Art. Most of the ones whom Sam had already secured for the exhibition were from out of state. This prompted him to concentrate on finding some quality, local artists who would fit the genre. He used all his search tools on the Internet and selected three local artists who either specialized in Pop Art or in a compatible genre.

Now he had to conjure up a name for the exhibition that would draw interest. After three glasses of Chardonnay and some deliberation, Charles had a brilliant idea.

Andy Warhol was the godfather of Pop Art. Everyone has heard of him. If he were alive today, what kind of Pop Art would Warhol be doing?

Charles named the exhibition *What Would Andy Do?*. Now that he had a name, it was past time to prepare a press release. He checked his iPhone for the time. It was 1:00 a.m. The media would have to wait until tomorrow.

* * *

CHARLES SPENT THE better part of the next morning drafting a formal press release. When he was satisfied with the final product, he fired it off in an email to Sam. Although she had not requested final approval, Charles felt it only appropriate.

Sam sent an immediate reply expressing her endorsement of and excitement about the name. She ended it with the sentence, *Let the Andy Warhol hordes descend upon the Trinity River Gallery.*

That afternoon, Charles loaded up his FIAT Spider with as many of his paintings as he could find. To squeeze into his trunk, no painting could exceed thirty inches in all directions. He pulled up to The Wine Therapist precisely at 3:00 p.m. and parked next to Rachel's Hyundai, locked his car, and walked inside. When he opened the door, the familiar scrape of metal-on-metal chafed his ears. Rachel stood behind the bar with an empty glass and two bottles of Chardonnay resting on the bar in front of her.

"Rachel," Charles called out, "are you *ever* going to get that front door fixed?"

"No way. It adds to the ambiance of the place."

"If you say so." He jerked his thumb over his shoulder. "Is it all right if I start bringing in the paintings?"

"Sure, I'll help you. But first, come over here and taste these two Chardonnays."

Rachel hid the label on the bottles, poured a small amount from one of them into a glass, and handed the glass to Charles. He performed the obligatory sniff, swirled the wine, then took a small sip. "Not bad. Not as oaky as I like."

She disposed of the first glass and poured a tasteful from the second bottle into a new glass. Charles repeated the ritual and took a sip. "Now this is more like it."

"You're so damn predictable. I knew you would select the California wine over the French one." She turned the bottles around.

Without glancing at the labels, Charles smiled. "I know what I like. Shall we unload the paintings?"

The Wine Therapist did not open to the public until 4:00 p.m. They both spent an hour hanging art and drinking wine. Charles sat at the end of the bar, his usual spot when he had been a frequent patron, admiring his newly hung paintings while Rachel visited with a woman and man at the opposite end. Charles recognized the couple as regulars.

After a few exchanges of pleasantries, Rachel walked back over to where Charles was seated. "Would you like another glass?"

He stared down at his glass, debating whether or not to get another. "No, I better not. I need to do some work when I get back to my apartment."

"Work? I didn't think you did anything but paint these days."

"I'm curating the next exhibition at the gallery." He stared at her and gave her a slow blink of disbelief.

"Are you serious?"

"I'm afraid so. The owner of the gallery asked me

if I would cover for her. She has to take care of her former partner, who is having some medical issues."

"What kind of exhibition do you plan?"

"Pop Art."

"I love Pop Art. When does it open?"

"In three weeks on a Saturday night."

"Crap!" She pounded her fist on the bar. "I have to work Saturday nights."

"With a lot of luck, I'll have all the art hung a couple of days in advance. You can come down during the day and see it then."

"How about I come down the Friday before the opening, and you can treat me to dinner afterward? I take every other Friday off now.

"Sure." He crinkled the corner of one eye. "Sounds good."

When Rachel saw his expression, she guffawed. "Don't act so surprised, Charles. It's *only* dinner."

"Let's just hope I'm able to get all the art from the artists and finish curating the exhibition before then." He stood up. "Well, I'm off."

She walked around from behind the bar. "Not without a hug before you leave."

Charles smiled. "Of course. I wouldn't skip it for the world."

CHAPTER 31

Only three more days until the opening of *What Would Andy Do?*. Charles had just finished breakfast and was enjoying a cup of coffee, sitting in his living room gazing at downtown Dallas, when his cell phone vibrated on his kitchen counter.

He rushed to pick it up and a wave of nausea washed over him. Detective Gonzales's name flashed on his phone's screen. "Hello, Detective."

"Hello, Pierce. We have a potential break in the Reverchon Park case."

He eased onto one of the bar stools in his kitchen. "I take it that the fact you're calling instead of showing up at my apartment to arrest me is good news."

"Don't get too excited. You're not off the hook yet."

"Of course not," Charles said in a voice laden with sarcasm. "That would be too good to be true."

"I need you to come down to headquarters."

"Detective, I'm curating an exhibition at the Trinity River Gallery that's opening this Saturday. I still have a million things to do. Can this wait until next Monday?"

The detective cleared his throat. "The longer we wait, Pierce, the more likely another crime will be committed and your business card possibly being found at the scene."

"When do want me down there?"

"This afternoon at 3:00 p.m."

Charles sighed. "I'll be there, Detective."

"With all the practice you've had, I'm sure you know where to go."

"Yes."

"Bye, Pierce."

Charles hung up his phone.

* * *

CHARLES TEXTED SAM from the parking lot next to the Dallas Police Department headquarters to let her know he would be delayed in coming to the gallery that afternoon. She hadn't shown up for two weeks while taking care of Simone. As he waited for Detective Gonzales, he received a return text from Sam indicating she would try to drop by the gallery early in the evening.

Detective Gonzales rounded the corner. "Thanks for coming, Pierce. We'll be in room 9 on the left. Go inside, and I'll be back in a few minutes."

Charles took a seat at the table. He wondered if the detective would read him his Miranda rights again. The door opened, and Detective Gonzales came inside carrying a file and a thick binder. He dropped them both on the table and sat down across from Charles.

"As I indicated on the phone," Detective Gonzales

said, "we have a viable break in the case. Do you remember me telling you about the amateur sleuth and his dog who conducted their own investigation?"

"Yes."

"As you recall, several weeks had passed between when the body was found and the date the man and his dog discovered the weapon. Forensics discovered two sets of DNA on the wrench and matched one set to the deceased woman. The other set matches a man in the database who has a criminal record as long as my arm. It's unlikely, but at least possible, this man didn't commit the crime. He might have stumbled across the wrench in the park and picked it up to determine if it was of any value to him. With his record, though, he's our primary suspect."

"That's definitely good news for *me*. So am I no longer a suspect?"

Detective Gonzales reached for the binder. "Let's just say you're not the primary suspect." He rifled through some pages. The binder contained photographs of row after row of men. "Pierce, are you acquainted with a David Wayne Stapler?"

Charles paused to let the question register. "No, I don't think I've ever heard of a David Wayne Stapler."

"This is a mug shot of him." Detective Gonzales turned the binder around. It contained a profile and a straight-on picture of a man with dark hair who appeared to be in his late twenties or early thirties. "Have you seen this man?"

Charles studied the mug shots. "I'm not totally

sure I've seen him before—

"Could he be the man who threatened you in your studio?"

"I was going to say just that. He *does* resemble that guy."

"But you're not one hundred percent certain?"

"That's correct. I would say I'm about eighty percent."

Detective Gonzales closed the book. "If you again saw that guy who threatened you, do you think you'd recognize him?"

"I'm sure I would." Charles leaned forward. "Have you arrested this Stapler character?"

"Not yet. He has an outstanding warrant for breaking his bail requirements in an unrelated matter. He's elusive as hell."

"Under the circumstances, is it safe to assume the DA will *not* present a case against me to the grand jury for indictment?"

"Unless something else ties you to the homicide," the detective said with a blank look, "that's a safe assumption."

"Do you believe it was Stapler who tried to shoot me outside the gallery?"

Gonzales slumped in his chair. "It's possible. We haven't gotten anything new in that matter."

Charles pondered whether to tell him that Simone owned a pistol which could have fired those bullets. "Detective, didn't you tell me forensics found that the bullet lodged into the gallery wall belonged to a

German pistol?"

"That's right. Why do you ask?"

"Do you remember the exact type of pistol?"

Frowning, Detective Gonzales studied him. "I would have to check the file. Why the sudden interest in German weaponry?"

"If you were shot at, wouldn't you want to know what type of pistol was used?"

"Pierce, I'm a detective. I've been shot at on numerous occasions. I could care less what kind of gun was used. My only concern was that I wasn't hit by a bullet."

"I can appreciate that. But I've never been targeted before, so I really would like to know what kind of pistol was used."

"All right, Pierce, I'll check on it and get back with you."

"Thank you, Detective."

Gonzales stood up. "That's all for now. You're free to go."

* * *

AFTER LEAVING POLICE headquarters, Charles drove through downtown Dallas in the direction of the Trinity River Gallery. It was the beginning of rush-hour traffic, so it took him almost forty-five minutes to drive the short distance to the Design District. He heaved a sigh of relief to see Sam's car parked in front. He unlocked the front door and relocked it behind him.

Sam appeared from the back of the gallery. "You've been busy, Charles. The gallery's looking good."

"Thanks. I would've been almost finished hanging the art, except that I had to go downtown to meet Detective Gonzales."

"What did the detective want this time?"

"The weapon used in the homicide of that woman in Reverchon Park was found. Forensics discovered two sets of DNA on it. One set belongs to the victim, and the other matches some guy in the police database."

Her expression turned cheerful. "Does that mean they've taken you off the suspect list in the case?"

"Unfortunately, not quite. At least this other guy is the primary suspect, instead of me."

Sam smiled. "Well, that's progress, anyway."

"I apologize for not asking earlier, but how's Simone doing?"

"She's recovering nicely. In fact, I'll be back part-time to work in the gallery tomorrow and can help you finish getting everything ready for the opening."

Making a fist, Charles held up one thumb. "That's cause for a celebratory glass of wine."

Sam giggled. "Agreed. Let's have it here and talk about what still needs to be done."

Charles returned with two glasses of wine. "I made a safe assumption you would prefer a nice Cabernet Sauvignon over Chardonnay."

"Perfect, thanks."

"By the way, Sam, I had a novel experience today. I got to review mug shots at the police department."

Sam grinned. "That's definitely something I've never experienced. Was that in relation to the new suspect they have in the Reverchon case?"

"Yes, the guy is named David Wayne Stapler. Has it ever occurred to you how many notorious criminals have *Wayne* as a middle name?"

Sam rolled her eyes. "I guess I haven't really thought about it. By the way, what's your middle name, Charles?"

Charles laughed. "Sanders. Not very exciting, is it?"

"It doesn't sound too threatening." Sam hesitated. "What did you say was this Wayne guy's last name?"

"Stapler. Why?"

"That's the last name of the former director of CDADA who was stealing money from the association. Remember? Her name is Cindy Stapler."

The name association sent a chill down Charles's spine. "Cindy Stapler got prosecuted for stealing CDADA's funds. Didn't one of the board members say her son had mental issues and she used the funds to bail him out of jail?"

"Yes, Charles. Her son apparently has had a lot of problems with the law."

"Remember that strange guy who threatened me in my studio?"

"Yes."

"He blamed me for getting his family in trouble. He must be David Wayne Stapler and somehow learned I was the attorney who advised the CDADA board on the matter."

Sam grimaced. "But you only recommended to the board that Cindy reimburse CDADA for the funds she misappropriated. You never suggested that anyone should notify the police."

Charles took a drink of wine. "That's true. But he must have made that connection and held me responsible. Maybe Stapler confronted one of the board members, and they passed the buck and told him I was responsible for getting his mother arrested."

"He has had so much trouble with the law," Sam said, "he's probably distrustful of all attorneys."

"That's likely true. On the other hand, it may be just a coincidence that David Wayne and Cindy have the same last name. I suppose Stapler is not that uncommon a name. Nevertheless, the man who threatened me specifically mentioned that I got his family into trouble. I'm going to call Detective Gonzales in the morning."

Sam set her glass down on the bar. "It's getting a little late. Let's wait until tomorrow to do anything further with getting the gallery ready for the opening."

"Sounds good. I'll be here in the morning to begin working again."

"Great, thanks."

"Sam, are you okay talking with Detective Gonzales if I can get him down here sometime tomorrow?"

"Sure, if I can be of any help."

Charles was on Cloud Nine.

Finally, I'll be able to put all this trouble behind me! Maybe I can quit worrying that someone wants to kill me.

CHAPTER 32

Charles contacted Detective Gonzales right after breakfast and gave him a brief description of his suspicions about David Wayne Stapler. The detective agreed to come to the Trinity River Gallery to meet with him and Sam at 3:00 p.m.

Charles pulled his FIAT Spider up to the Trinity River Gallery at 10:00 a.m. The parking in front was vacant except for his car. He let himself inside and relocked the front door.

An hour later, Charles hung the last painting for the exhibition. The front buzzer rang, and seconds later, Sam emerged from the front of the gallery and entered the back part where Charles was working. "It looks like you're about finished," she said.

"Unless you would like to change the position of some of the art, the hanging part is done. I still have to adjust the lighting."

Sam toured the entire gallery and suggested only one change. Except for a quick break to down a sandwich, Charles spent the rest of the morning and early afternoon adjusting the lighting. When he was satisfied, he went to Sam's office.

She looked up as he approached her door. "All done with the lights?"

"I think it's done, but I'm sure you want to double-check to make certain no further changes are needed."

"No, that's fine, Charles. By the way, excellent job on the PR. We're getting some good press coverage of the exhibition."

"Really? Which outlets?"

"The *Dallas Morning News* gave us a mention online, the *Dallas Observer*, and *Dallas Art News*. That should generate some interest."

The front door to the gallery buzzed, and Charles popped his head out of Sam's office. Detective Gonzales entered the gallery and paused to look at a small painting Charles had hung minutes earlier. The painting depicted a nude woman climbing out of a Campbell's Soup can. It was a tribute to Warhol. He shot a glance over at Charles. "Now, this kind of art, I understand."

"Come around often enough, Detective, and you'll find something you like."

Sam emerged from her office. "Hello, Detective, good to see you again."

Charles remembered Sam was in the gallery the day Detectives Gonzales and Grayson had arrested him.

"Thank you. I'm happy I don't have to arrest anyone here today." Detective Gonzales chuckled. "Unless, of course, you tell me something that changes my mind."

"Detective," Charles said, "do you want to meet

with both of us at once or individually?"

"I think we can save some time and meet all together."

Sam said, "Let's go into my conference room, then."

After they were settled, Charles said, "Shall I begin?"

"Go for it," Detective Gonzales said.

"As I indicated on the phone, I think Sam and I might have connected this David Wayne Stapler with the man who threatened me in my studio. I didn't tell you this part before because I didn't think it was relevant to your investigation."

Expressionless, the detective nodded.

"Anyway, I provided some legal advice to the Contemporary Dallas Art Dealers Association board of directors. Sam sits on the board. The board discovered the managing director had been stealing funds from the association. That theft, though no fault of the association, could threaten CDADA's tax-exempt status. My advice to the board was that it must have Cindy Stapler reimburse the funds or face consequences from the—"

"Did you say her last name was Stapler?" Detective Gonzales took out his notepad.

Sam said, "Yes, her full name is Cindy Stapler. The board was made aware that she used these funds to post bail for her son. He evidently has a long criminal history."

"Do you remember, Detective," Charles said, "I

told you this man accused me of getting his family in trouble? I believe he was going to become violent that night until Sam's timely appearance."

"Fortunately," Sam said, "I seemed to spook him, and he abruptly left."

"As you recall, Sam, when he left," Charles said, "he grabbed my business cards and other stuff off the shelf next to the door. He trashed the hallway outside of my studio. It's possible he pocketed some of my cards."

She nodded. "That's correct."

"This guy," said Charles, "whether or not it's Stapler, was probably the culprit who planted my business card at all the crime scenes."

"Pierce," said Detective Gonzales, "did you advise the board to call the police on his mother?" He clicked his pen twice.

"No, I didn't say anything involving the police. My advice was limited to having Cindy reimburse the association to avoid adverse tax consequences."

"Until the board learned of the possible tax problems," Sam said, "everyone was pretty much sympathetic toward Cindy's plight as a single mother with a problem son. It wasn't until later that the board decided to contact the police. Charles was not involved in any of those discussions."

Detective Gonzales sighed. "Pierce, why do you think Stapler thought you were responsible for having his mother arrested?"

"That's the only disconnect. I don't know,

unless one of the board members told Stapler I was responsible."

"Perhaps David Wayne Stapler threatened one of board members," Sam said, "and he or she implicated Charles."

Detective Gonzales nodded. "That's a plausible explanation. Any idea who that might have been?"

"I don't know. Some on the board were more vocal than others about going to the police. However, that doesn't mean this guy contacted any of them."

Detective Gonzales, "Okay, this information is helpful. Anything else?"

"That's all I know to tell you." Charles glanced at Sam. "Can you think of anything further?"

"No."

Detective Gonzales rose halfway but plopped down again. "I almost forgot. I checked the file for the kind of pistol that shot the bullet extracted from the gallery wall." He reached into his coat pocket and pulled out a piece of paper.

Charles stared at Sam.to observe her expression when the detective identified the pistol that was used. How would she react if it turned out to be the type of gun Simone owned?

Detective Gonzales squinted to read the paper. "It was a German nine-millimeter semiautomatic pistol produced from 1978 to 2008 by Heckler & Koch."

Sam perked up. "Did you say a German-made pistol?"

"That's correct. They aren't commonly found in

America."

"That's interesting. My ex owns a German P38 nine-millimeter pistol that she inherited."

Detective Gonzales gave her a wry smile. "Well, I guess we have at least two different types of German pistols in Dallas, then."

"So police forensics was able to identify the precise type of pistol that fired the bullet?"

"Yes, in some instances, and that was the case here."

Charles remained silent. He would have bet a fortune that Simone was the culprit.

Detective Gonzales stood up. "Stay safe, folks. Thanks for the information."

After he was gone, Charles said, "Are you relieved to find out Simone was not the one who shot at me?"

"I know you had your suspicions, but I never thought she was the one. As I said before, she's an excellent shot. She would never shoot at anyone, no matter the circumstances. However, if she did shoot, she wouldn't miss."

"Now, to change the subject on purpose," Charles said, "the opening is the day after tomorrow. What else needs to be done?"

"I need to confirm with Mary that she has the wine ready for pick up tomorrow, but that should be it."

"Great. I may actually do some painting in my studio tomorrow."

Charles took a deep breath, a steady one for the

first time since the shooting.

Thank God, I was wrong about Simone. Stapler's got to be the shooter, and now the police have more incriminating information on him. He exhaled. *My troubles are all but over.*

CHAPTER 33

A t 4:15 p.m., Charles was in his studio when the front door buzzed in the distance. He had only arrived about thirty minutes before, after deciding to take the day off from any responsibilities.

Her high heels clicking against the concrete floor, Rachel strutted through his studio door dressed in a black top and slacks. Her face lit up when she saw Charles. "I absolutely love the art!" she said. "I got just a glimpse as I was wandering back here."

"Thanks. Shall we get a glass of wine and go explore?"

"What excellent bottle are you serving back here in a red?"

"I just stocked up for tomorrow night. Not sure why, since I will probably be helping Sam out front. I may not be able to spend much time entertaining back here."

Rachel scanned his red wine inventory. "How about the Ramey Cabernet?"

"Sounds good. I'm going to have their Chardonnay myself."

Charles poured them each a glass, and they headed down the hallway to the rear part of the gallery.

As Charles gave Rachel a tour of the exhibition, Sam turned on some electronic dance music and shouted across the gallery floor, "What do you think about this genre of music for tomorrow night?"

Charles whirled around. "It's perfect for early in the event. But we have to play some Velvet Underground later in the evening, though. After all, the group was Andy Warhol's house band at the Factory."

Sam lowered the volume. "Brilliant idea!"

Charles said, "Sam, I want you to meet a good friend of mine."

Sam crossed the room to join Charles and Rachel.

Charles placed a hand on each woman's upper arm, then turned toward Sam. "This is Rachel. She's my favorite therapist."

Sam said, "Please to meet you, Rachel."

"Likewise."

"Just so you know," Charles said, "Rachel manages The Wine Therapist."

Sam smiled. "Your favorite treatment."

"Most definitely."

Sam turned aside. "I'll leave you two to enjoy the exhibit."

"Charles," Rachel said, "didn't you paint anything for the exhibition?"

He grinned. "Yes, I did something Pop Art but uniquely Texas."

"Where is it?"

Charles pointed to the opposite side of the gallery.

"It's that triptych over there."

He followed Rachel over to his painting, a figurative work that depicted a woman sucking on one end of a straw. The other end was buried in a can of Ranch Style Beans.

"What's it called?"

Charles snickered. "*Appetite Pleasin'.*"

Rachel examined the painting up close. "How is it uniquely Texas?"

"Ranch Style Beans are only manufactured in Texas. It's my attempted version of Andy Warhol's Campbell Soup can."

Rachel laughed. "I get it. That's very clever!"

"Thank you."

They continued to tour the gallery, checking out the various takes on contemporary Pop Art, including an experimental short-film screening in Sam's conference room that involved rolling soup cans.

"I made reservations for dinner at 7:00 p.m. at Stephan Pyles," Charles said. "Would you like to go early and get a drink at the bar?"

"Great idea."

Charles locked his studio. As they walked past her office, Charles called out to Sam, "Good night. We're off to dinner."

"Good night," she called out. "Enjoy."

He and Rachel exited the gallery, and Charles locked the door behind them. "Would you like to ride with me to the restaurant?"

She smirked. "Well, I'll either have to ride with

you or else walk."

"How did you get here?"

"Lyft. I use them all the time when I know I'm going to be drinking."

Charles laughed. "So you're pretty certain you'll be drinking a lot, then."

Rachel raised one eyebrow and winked at him. "Just being prepared."

Charles unlocked the passenger side of his FIAT Spider. Before he opened the door for her, he said, "The Spider is fun as hell to drive, but I'm afraid it's really a one-seater."

She stared inside through the window. "Not a lot of legroom on the passenger side."

"That's correct. The gas tank takes up most of it."

Rachel managed to slide her long legs inside while Charles climbed into the driver's side. He chuckled when her knees tucked up almost up to her chin. "It's not a long drive."

The valet recognized Charles from a previous visit. He parked the Spider in front of the restaurant in between a Lamborghini and a Lexus SC 430.

While waiting at the bar to get a drink, Charles gestured toward the front window of the restaurant. "I discovered long ago that it pays to tip well. See where the valet parked the Spider."

"You didn't tell me," said Rachel, "you were a VIP."

"I'm a VIP *only* in the eyes of the guys who park the cars. Not with anyone else, I assure you."

They enjoyed cocktails at the bar and then were seated at a prime table near the wall. Rachel said, "It looks to me like you got a VIP table."

"Yes, I wonder why."

They had a wonderful dinner and split a bottle of Flowers Chardonnay. Charles was feeling the effects of the alcohol and suspected Rachel sensed no pain either. She suggested another cocktail at the bar following dinner. Charles convinced her he was fine to drive her home, but one more might put him over the edge.

Rachel lived in a quaint, small 1940s bungalow just east of the Central Expressway. Although she was tipsy, she was able to navigate Charles through the winding, tree-lined streets. A glance in his rearview mirror revealed a car was tailing him. "God, I hope that's not a police car."

"Is someone following us?"

"I saw this car right after we crossed the Central Expressway on Henderson. Since then, he's kept up with every move we've made."

When Charles turned onto Rachel's street, he pulled over to the side and parked. She said, "This isn't my house."

"I didn't think it was. I'm just checking to see if we're still being followed."

Charles waited five minutes before inching away from the curb. There was no sign of the car. "I guess I was mistaken."

"My house is on the corner to the left."

He stopped in front, pondering what was going to happen next.

Rachel swung open her door. "Come on, Charles. Walk me to the door."

Charles locked the Spider and followed her up the uneven sidewalk that neighboring oak tree roots had cracked and lifted over the decades. Rachel stumbled but caught herself. Charles managed to make it to the front porch without tripping. After she dropped her keys trying to unlock the front door, he picked them up and unlocked it for her.

Rachel walked inside, and Charles waited on the front porch. When he did not follow her, she said, "Come in for a while, and lock the door behind you."

He stepped across the threshold. She walked over to him and whispered, "You're not going anywhere tonight."

* * *

CHARLES WOKE UP on his back at 5:00 a.m. He lay in bed trying to focus his gaze on the ceiling. The light fixture over the bed was unfamiliar.

Charles felt movement in the bed to his right and remembered what had transpired. He lay still for two more hours, not wanting to disturb Rachel. Never in his wildest imagination had he ever expected to sleep with her.

My God, this'll be so awkward when she wakes up. What are the expectations going forward?

Rachel rolled over and opened her eyes. She smiled, then murmured, "Are you still here?"

"Yes, I'm still here."

"Don't worry. Last night was fun, but nothing has changed between us. We're still just friends."

Not knowing how to respond, Charles said, "Would you like me to make breakfast?"

"No, I'm going back to sleep. Please lock the front door on your way out."

"Will do."

I slept with Rachel? He crawled out of bed and bent down to pick up his clothes off the floor. *I'm not ready for a relationship yet.*

He tiptoed toward the bedroom door, then turned around to stare at her sleeping figure. *What did she mean when she said we were still just friends?*

CHAPTER 34

Charles arrived two hours before the opening on Saturday night. Neither Sam nor Mary had showed up yet.

Everything needed perfect staging. He flipped on all the lights in the gallery and walked around straightening paintings and checking the label position by each piece that listed the title, medium, and price. Satisfied, he went back to Studio 1 to prepare it for the evening.

Charles was energized, still riding a high from the night spent with Rachel. He opened his refrigerator, pulled out a bottle of Rombauer Chardonnay, popped the cork, and poured a glass for himself.

The buzzer of the front door sounded. A few minutes later, music played in the gallery. Either Sam or Mary had arrived. He wandered to the front of the gallery, pausing to check his art on the exterior of Studio 1.

Sam appeared around the corner. "I see you're already enjoying some wine."

Charles laughed. "Yes, I'm celebrating that the gallery looks damn good and that we have worked our asses off to make this exhibition successful."

"In that case, I'll join you."

As they ambled back inside Studio 1 to get Sam a glass of wine, she said, "Are you sure you're not celebrating last night's dinner with your beautiful dinner date?"

Charles felt his face flush. "To be honest, it was a very enjoyable evening. I can't remember when I've had a better time."

"Where'd you go for dinner?"

"Stephan Pyles."

"If dinner was that good, I guess I'll have to make reservations there soon. However, I suspect from the look on your face that dinner was a minor part of the evening."

Charles did not respond but shook his head as if in playful disbelief regarding what Sam may have implied. To change the subject, he said, "Is Mary here yet?"

"Okay, I won't pry into your private life. Yes, she came in the same time I did."

"Good. I anticipate the crowd will arrive early for this exhibition."

The opening was scheduled to begin at 7:00 p.m. By 6:45 p.m., a stream of people had already filed into the gallery. The experimental film seemed to be garnering a lot of attention. People were huddled around the entrance to Sam's conference room where it was screening.

As the night progressed, the guests shifted from young, art student types to more of the beautiful crowd. Mary kept busy at the bar, pouring wine. From time to time, Charles checked with her to make sure she was not overwhelmed. Sam did her gallery owner duties by asking people who appeared to be viewing the art if they had any questions. On occasion, she disappeared into her office to collect some information on an artist or to get a red dot for a painting label that signified a sale had been made.

Charles decided to check on Studio 1 to see if he had any visitors. As soon as he walked inside, three women were finishing off his bottle of Rombauer Chardonnay he had been chilling. Without saying a word, he pulled another bottle from his refrigerator, popped the cork, and set it on the coffee table. The Rombauer Zinfandel was still about half full.

In his own Studio 1, Charles was content to be part-resident artist and part-waiter. After performing his waiter obligations, he poured himself a glass of Chardonnay and then headed back to the gallery.

The crowd in the gallery was near capacity, which meant only one thing: it was prime time. Charles scooted over to the bar to check on Mary. The group clustered in front of the bar had grown as well. He walked behind it to help her serve wine.

As he handed a woman a glass of Chardonnay, a familiar voice said, "Is this as good as the wine served in Studio 1?"

Charles jerked his head up. Jamie Simon stood in front of him, flashing a sinister smile. She was dressed in an expensive black suit and light-gray blouse.

"Jamie, so nice of you to come," he said. "To be very candid, I didn't expect to see you again."

Her smile vanished. "I came here *strictly* to see the art."

When the crowd thinned at the bar, Mary said, "Thanks, I can handle it now, Charles."

Jamie was standing by herself at one of the cocktail tables interspersed throughout the gallery. Charles walked over to her. "May I get you a nice glass of Chardonnay from my studio? Judging by your full glass, it obviously wasn't to your liking."

She feigned a smile. "I'll wait patiently for you to return."

Charles set his glass of wine on the table. "I'll be back in a few minutes."

Studio 1 was packed. Every inch of Charles's couch was occupied, as well as his guest chairs. A woman had plopped in the chair by his easel, a glass of wine in one hand and one of Charles's paintbrushes in the other. When he approached, she set the brush down and said, "Oh, sorry."

"That's quite all right," Charles said, "as long as you don't have paint on your brush." He extracted a bottle of Frank Family Chardonnay from the refrigerator, popped the cork, and exited his studio without addressing anyone else. He surmised that the group in Studio 1 had had enough wine.

Jamie still stood at the table. She had rested her purse on top of it next to Charles's wine glass. He walked around the bar and retrieved two empty glasses, then set them on the tabletop and poured wine in each of them.

"Aren't you going to finish the glass you already poured yourself?" she said.

The sight of Jamie's purse next to his wine glass had again triggered Charles's memory of when she had pretended to poison him on the cruise. "This is a different Chardonnay than what I was previously drinking."

"Still don't trust me, do you?"

She was correct. Charles could not bring himself to trust her. "That's not it. I just don't like to mix different types of Chardonnay."

In a voice loaded with sarcasm, Jamie said, "I'm *sure* that's the reason. If you'll excuse me, I'm going to check out the art." She walked away from the table to the front of the gallery.

Charles cleared the table and put the bottle of Frank Family Chardonnay in the refrigerator behind the bar.

Sam approached him and said, "This is prime time for sales."

"What do you mean?" Charles said. "The crowd is half the size it was only a few minutes ago."

"That's exactly right. It needs to be less frantic for potential buyers to feel comfortable. By now, they've consumed the right amount of alcohol to fortify the decision to make the plunge and buy a piece."

As if on cue, a woman approached her. "Are you Sam?"

"Yes, may I help you?"

"My husband and I are interested in the piece on the front wall in the gallery."

Sam shot Charles an 'I told you so' glance. "Let's go up front and talk about it."

Charles decided to go back and check on Studio 1. The hordes had cleared out. With no more wine open to fuel them, they had no reason to hang around there. When Charles returned to the gallery, he spotted Jamie seated at the bar engaged in conversation with a muscular, handsome man.

Although Jamie was very attractive, she seemed flattered by drawing the attention of the young man. Every time Charles wandered into the vicinity, they were downing another glass.

Charles speculated she had learned to tolerate the wine served in the gallery. He went behind the bar and poured himself a glass of Frank Family Chardonnay. It was a good excuse to talk to Mary. Neither Jamie nor the man noticed his presence.

Charles whispered, "Mary, I don't think it's wise to serve them any more wine."

"I agree. I'm just not sure how to handle the situation."

"Let me assume the bartending duties, and you can go take a break."

Mary nodded and left. Charles cleared the wine bottles from the bar and glasses from the bar area.

"Hey, dude," the man said, "what did you do with the wine?"

Jamie glared at Charles.

Ad-libbing, Charles said, "Sorry, we have to stop serving alcohol at this time of night."

The man slurred, "Sssseriousssly?"

"I'm afraid so. That's the law." Charles hoped the man did not call his bluff.

The man took one final swig from his glass and slammed it down on the bar. "I'm outta here."

Jamie grabbed his arm. "Shall we go somewhere else?"

In a flash, the man jerked his arm away from her. "*We* ain't going *anywhere* together."

"Why? I didn't do anything wrong."

The man stood up and stomped to the front of the gallery and out the door.

Charles said, "Good riddance."

Jamie rested her head on the bar, put her hands over her head, and sobbed.

Charles was not sure whether to comfort her or give her some space. After a moment, he said, "Are you all right?"

She did not respond but continued to sob. Charles decided to leave her alone. He walked into the front of the gallery and spotted Sam saying good night to a couple. Sam turned around and headed toward her office when Charles motioned for her. "What's up?"

"You know the woman who tried to poison me?"

"You mean the woman," Sam said in an acerbic tone, "whom you also took to dinner?"

Charles grimaced. "Yes, she's back there with her

head lying on the bar, crying."

Sam studied his expression, frowning at first, then her face muscles relaxed. "What did you do to the poor woman?"

With a shrug, Charles lifted his hands as high as his ears. "I didn't *do* anything. She and a man were at the bar drinking way too much. So I stepped in for Mary and told them we couldn't serve them any more wine. That agitated the man, and he stormed out of the gallery, leaving Jamie by herself."

Sam nodded and whispered, "She's behind you."

Jamie's face was flushed, as tears streamed down her cheeks. She marched past them toward the front door.

Charles shouted, "Wait, Jamie!"

She exited the gallery, and Charles sprinted after her. He caught up with her half a block down the sidewalk. He laid a gentle hand on her shoulder and said, "Please at least let me walk you to your car."

Jamie did not respond but did not resist either. Charles walked beside her. She had difficulty maintaining her balance.

"You appear a little bit tipsy. Why don't we call Lyft or Uber?"

"I'm fine. Leave me alone."

"Let me drive you home then."

"Not a chance in hell, Charles." Jamie pulled her key remote out of her purse and pressed it several times. "Where's my damn car?"

A block away, her Lexus SUV's taillights blinked.

"It's just up the street on the other side," he said as he pointed to the opposite curb.

When they reached her car, Charles made one final plea for her not to drive, but she was determined. He waited as she eased her car away from the curb and crept out of sight down Levee Street.

Sam had observed from the front door of the gallery. When Charles drew closer, she said, "Didn't you try to stop her?"

"I did, Sam. She was belligerent and hell-bent on driving. I didn't want to force her keys out of her hand."

"I hope she gets home safely."

"Me, too."

When they were back in the gallery, Sam gave him a kiss on the cheek.

His eyes widened as he smiled. "Not that I minded, but what was that for?"

"From a sales perspective, this was the best opening we've ever had. Thank you, Mr. Pierce, for curating the exhibition."

"You're most welcome," Charles said. "I would offer you a celebratory glass of wine, but I won't be able to join you because I have had my limit."

"No problem. I think enough wine has already been served here tonight."

He laughed. "I only hope the sales you made cover the cost of all the wine consumed."

Sam grinned. "You forget, the gallery doesn't serve that expensive stuff you pour in Studio 1. By the way, did you sell any of your art?"

"No, I was only able to sneak back there a few times. The folks in my studio downed several bottles of my finest wine, though."

Mary emerged from Sam's office. "All the sales information is entered into the system, Sam."

"Great. Thanks, Mary."

"I didn't realize you were still here," said Charles.

"Yes, but I'm heading out now. Thanks, Charles, for covering for me at the bar with that drunk couple."

The three of them left the gallery together. As usual, Charles checked his email while waiting for Sam and Mary to drive away. He started up the FIAT Spider and headed south on Levee Street. He then took a left onto Oak Lawn Avenue. There was little traffic this time of night.

Charles stopped at a red light at the intersection of Oak Lawn Avenue and Market Center Boulevard. Flashing, red lights were reflected in the windows on the other side of Market Center Boulevard.

When the light changed to green, Charles edged forward into the intersection. To his left parked behind a black SUV was a police car with its lights flashing.

Damn, I hope that's not Jamie!

CHAPTER 35

N ow that the opening of *What Would Andy Do?* was in the rearview mirror, Charles spent the following week painting in his studio.

Thursday afternoon, Charles decided to leave early and drive over to The Wine Therapist. He worried their first meeting would be a little awkward. He had not spoken to Rachel since they spent the night together almost a week ago.

A woman was standing in front of The Wine Therapist staring through the window. As Charles approached, she said, "Is this place open?"

"It should be. Why do you ask?"

"Because it looks dark inside."

Charles opened the door to the familiar scrape of metal. He held it open for the woman and followed her in. She paused at the row of wine bottles just to the left inside the entry. A couple was seated at the left side of the bar, so Charles made a beeline to the right side of the bar to his favorite stool at the end.

Rachel emerged from the small kitchen area behind the right side of the bar and straightaway went over to the woman. Charles pulled his phone out of his pocket to check his email. He jumped when Rachel approached from behind him and called out,

"Hello, Charles."

He dropped his phone on the bar.

"Afraid of your own name?" she said,

Charles laughed. "When you say it that loud, then I guess the answer would be yes."

Rachel strolled around to the other side of the bar without giving him a hug. This was the only time since they had first become friends that he could remember she did not hug him.

She brought over a bottle of Chardonnay. "I think you'll like this one. Have a taste." She poured a small amount into his glass.

Charles sniffed his glass and tasted the wine. "Pretty good. What kind is it?"

"Cakebread Reserve."

"I'm not sure I've ever tried this wine before."

"Excuse me," Rachel said, "I need to go check on the couple."

Charles watched her as she walked to the other side of the bar. He wondered if she would bring up the night they had spent together.

Rachel visited with the couple a few minutes and then returned to Charles's side of the bar. "I have some potential good news for you."

"I can use all the good news I can get."

"I say 'potential' because this guy who was kind of creepy came in the other evening around 9:00 p.m. When he first came through the door, I thought he was homeless. We sometimes have those people wander in here looking for a handout. Judging from this guy's appearance, he wasn't far removed from living on the streets."

She leaned on the back of the barstool next to him. "Before I could ask him if he would like to see the wine menu, he inquired whether the art on the walls was for sale. I told him yes. This guy then wanted to know the name of the artist. So I gave him your name. He asked me how much your *Burnt Orange Imperialism* piece cost. When I told him that the price label was next to the painting, he gave me a 'Go to hell' look and stomped over to read the label."

"Really? An almost homeless guy is interested in my art. Maybe he's some eccentric millionaire in disguise."

Rachel arched one eyebrow. "If that's true, he had a damn good disguise, not to mention his attitude."

"Did he leave after checking out the price?"

"No, he sat on the same stool where you're sitting and ordered a whiskey sour, of all things. I was almost afraid to tell him we serve only wine and beer. When I did, he muttered something under his breath and then ordered a beer. I brought him one, and he put seven dollars on the bar and told me to keep the change, which was twenty-five cents."

Charles smiled. "Big tipper, huh? I'm surprised anyone even notices the art exhibited here."

"That's what you always say, but I do sell some from time to time. By the way, how was the opening of the Pop Art exhibition?"

"We had an incredible turnout. Sam was pleased

because she racked up some sales. Oh, and get this, Jamie Simon showed up."

"You can't be serious." Rachel rested her palms on the edge of the bar and leaned forward.

"Yes, I'm serious. She got very intoxicated."

"Really?"

"She was flirting with some young guy, and they were downing the wine."

"She was probably flirting with him to make you jealous."

Charles snorted as he shook his head. "I've no idea what makes her tick. She's definitely an enigma."

Another woman came into The Wine Therapist and sat two barstools down from Charles. He halfway expected her to be Jamie. Charles shot a glance sideways but did not recognize her.

Rachel left to go wait on the woman. He listened as Rachel went through her spiel of explaining the wine menu to her.

Charles stared down at his empty glass. It was almost automatic for him to drink at least two, but he decided to have only one glass. Charles felt compelled to discuss with Rachel if there were any ramifications of their having slept together.

She saw his empty glass and picked up the bottle of Cakebread Chardonnay. Before she could refill his glass, Charles covered the top of it with his hand and said, "I'm just having one today."

"Are you sick?" she giggled.

He forced a smile. "No, I'm just not in the mood."

"Okay, let me get your check."

The check was for ten dollars, and Charles set down a twenty-dollar bill. Rachel said, "Would you like change?"

"You know I don't."

She walked around the bar to Charles's side. "Well, let me give you a hug before you leave."

Charles always loved hugging Rachel. He walked out of The Wine Therapist, unlocked his FIAT Spider, and slid into the driver's seat. Before he could start his car, his phone rang.

I wonder if that's Rachel.

It was Detective Gonzales. Staring at it, Charles let his phone ring several times before answering. "Hello, Detective."

"Pierce, I may have some good news for you."

"That's the second time someone has said that to me today," he chortled.

"What?"

"Nothing, sorry, Detective. What's this good news?"

"We think we may have the shooter."

Charles stared into the distance and frowned, letting the detective's word replay in his mind. "Are you referring to the person who tried to shoot me?"

"That's correct. We have a Heckler & Koch P7 that a patrol officer recovered when he was making an arrest the other night. Forensics needs to run more tests to determine if it's the exact pistol that shot at you."

"Very good, Detective. When will forensics complete the testing?"

"Great question. You never can tell with that group."

"I see. Thank you for letting me know."

"You're welcome. Bye, Pierce."

"Bye, Detective."

Charles sat for a minute. *Sounds like they have the gun and the shooter.* He turned the key in the ignition. *Now maybe I can get some answers and quit worrying that someone wants me dead.*

CHAPTER 36

At 3:00 p.m. the following day, Charles was sitting in his studio checking emails, when his phone chimed. He answered it. "Hey, Rachel."

"Hi. Charles. Are you painting?"

"No, I have been procrastinating. I'm just sitting on my couch in my studio, checking emails. What are you doing?"

"I just arrived at The Wine Therapist for work."

He waited until she unlocked the front door of the wine bar.

"What are you doing tonight?" she said.

"I don't have any plans." In the background, the distinct sound of metal scrapping metal told him someone had entered The Wine Therapist.

"Hold on. A customer just came in."

At the sound of a clang, Charles assumed Rachel had set her phone on top of the granite bar. He put his phone on speaker and turned the volume up.

A man's voice said, "Are you open?"

Rachel said, "Not officially until 4:00 p.m. I forgot to relock the door when I arrived."

The man said, "I see."

"Did you want something to drink?"

"I don't know. Let me think about it."

The man said, "You Pierce's girlfriend?"

"That's none of your business."

The man laughed. "I figured you to be his girlfriend since you've been sleeping with him."

Noise followed, indicating some commotion.

"Don't think I'm afraid to use this baseball bat," said Rachel. "You better leave now."

The man said in sneery voice, "Keep a bat under the bar, do you? You might live to regret threatening me."

Charles listened intently until the metal scraping of the front door opening sounded again. Then he screamed into the speaker of his phone, "Rachel, are you there?"

More noise, as Rachel picked up her phone. "Yes, that was scary! Did you hear our conversation?"

"Every word. Are you all right?"

"Just a little shaken but I'm fine."

"Who was that guy?"

"That creepy guy I told you about."

Charles frowned. "Which creepy guy are we talking about?"

"You know, the one I mentioned before, who was interested in your painting."

"The homeless-looking guy?"

"Yes. Listen, Charles, did you tell anyone we slept together?"

"Hell no!" he gasped. "I wouldn't ever do something like that. Why do you ask?"

"Because you heard the creepy guy ask me if I

was your girlfriend."

"I know. That's bizarre."

"He said he assumed I was your girlfriend because we've slept together."

"How the hell would he know that?"

"That's the million-dollar question, Charles!"

"Unless..." Charles snapped his fingers. "Do you remember when we were driving to your house from the restaurant and I thought someone might have been following us?"

Rachel sighed. "I don't remember a lot about that night."

Charles laughed. "Thanks, Rachel."

"I don't mean it like that. I just meant I had been overserved alcohol and don't recall getting home."

"Well, I was certain someone had followed us. After I turned onto your street, I pulled to the side of the road and waited to see if anyone came behind us. When no one did, I assumed I was mistaken. It's possible the creepy guy was following us then."

"But why?"

"I don't have an answer."

The door to The Wine Therapist scraped as it opened.

"I have to go, Charles," Rachel said, "I have a customer."

"Okay. Let's talk again soon. Be careful!"

"Always." Rachel hung up.

Charles spent the evening mulling over what Rachel had just experienced. *How many creepy guys are out there, ones who would give a damn who I slept with?* He paced in front of his window. *An old boyfriend? No, she would have recognized him. Who else would keep tabs on...* He stopped and stared at the horizon. *David Wayne Stapler!*

CHAPTER 37

Charles woke up early and stared at the ceiling of his apartment. After a restless night, he could not stop thinking about the creepy guy.

He forced himself out of bed, put on some sweats, and opened his apartment door to retrieve his newspaper. It was lying flat just outside his door. The headline of the lead story on page one was large enough for him to see without even picking it up. It read:

Woman's Body Found In Reverchon Park

Another body? I wonder if that's David Wayne Stapler's doing. Is Rachel next?

Charles made a cup of coffee and retired to his favorite Eames chair in the living room. The article described how a jogger had spotted the body in the underbrush near Turtle Creek just south of the Maple Avenue bridge.

As he read the article, he could not help but notice how similar the case was to the one involving the woman with the dog a few months earlier. The victim appeared to have been struck from behind with a blunt instrument, which was not found at the scene.

244 ◆ Jim Lively

Charles's phone rang on his nightstand. He set down the newspaper and hurried into his bedroom to answer it. Detective Gonzales's name was on the screen.

Not again! Surely, he's not contacting me about the body just found in Reverchon Park!

Charles hesitated, then answered before the call rolled to voice mail. "Hello, Detective."

"Sorry to call you so early, Pierce. But I need you to come down to headquarters today."

"Can you tell me what this is all about?"

"I have several things I need to discuss with you."

"What time, Detective?"

"3:00 p.m."

"I'll be there."

* * *

CHARLES ARRIVED AT Dallas Police Headquarters at 2:45 p.m. Similar to the previous times, he tapped his foot as he waited for the woman at the reception desk to acknowledge his presence. She glanced up at him and recognized him from his prior visits. "Here to see Detective Gonzales?"

"That's correct."

The woman placed a call to Detective Gonzales. When she hung up, she said, "You're in room 7. Down the hall to the left."

The door of the room was open, so Charles entered and sat in the chair opposite the door. Ten minutes later, Detective Gonzales entered the room, carrying a file, and shut the door behind him. He dropped it on the table in front of him. "Pierce, thank you for coming down here."

Charles nodded but did not say anything.

"This is what I call having a second bite of the apple."

"I don't follow you, Detective."

"Jamie Simon. Recognize that name?"

Charles's stomach twisted at the possible events Detective Gonzales would describe. He said, "Of course."

"She was arrested for suspicion of driving while intoxicated last Saturday night."

Charles groaned. "Damn it. I was afraid of that."

Detective Gonzales furrowed his brows. "What the hell does that mean?"

"Jamie attended an exhibition opening we had at the Trinity River Gallery. Over the course of the evening, she evidently had consumed too much—"

The detective held up his hand, palm forward. "Stop right there, Pierce. Did she know you were affiliated with the gallery?"

"Yes, Detective. It came out in my testimony at her trial that I was an artist. Jamie got on my website and discovered I had a studio at the gallery."

"Go on."

"Jamie attended an event at the gallery a few months earlier. She actually came in to see me."

"What the hell for?"

"She said she wanted to apologize because I was forced to testify against her."

Detective Gonzales slammed his fist on the table. "That's a crock of —"

"I thought so, too. But she seemed sincere."

"Have you forgotten that bitch tried to poison you, Pierce? How could you believe she was sincere?"

"I hear what you're saying, Detective, but she told me she had had therapy and was rehabilitated."

Detective Gonzales rolled his eyes. "You *believed* her?"

"Not really, except she was very convincing." Charles debated whether to tell the rest of the story but decided it was necessary. He continued. "She even purchased one of my paintings."

"To further substantiate her sincerity," Detective Gonzales said, "I suppose."

Charles lifted one shoulder in half a shrug. "I admit that was probably her plan."

"And now she's a regular visitor to the art gallery?"

"This next part you'll find hard to believe." Charles paused.

"Try me, Pierce."

"She met me for dinner at Fearing's."

Detective Gonzales groaned. "Pierce, has it ever occurred to you that maybe you are your own worst enemy?" He tsked-tsked. "When you play with fire, sometimes you get burned."

"I can appreciate your perspective, Detective, but I came out of the whole evening unscathed."

"Wasn't that the same evening someone left you a threatening note and a bullet with your apartment's valet?"

"Yes, but I don't think it was Jamie Simon."

"Do you remember I started this conversation by saying sometimes you have a second bite of the apple?"

"Yes."

"Would it surprise you to find out that Jamie was the owner of Heckler & Koch P7 pistol? The same type of pistol that fired the bullets at you, one of which was recovered from the gallery wall?"

Charles's jaw dropped, "Oh, my God."

"When she was arrested on suspicion of DWI, a Heckler & Koch P7 pistol was found in her purse. You may not be surprised to learn that she does not have a permit to carry a firearm."

"So the second bite of the apple," Charles said, one side of his mouth twisting up, "would be the chance to convict her of another crime, since she walked away free from the murder charge."

"That's it precisely."

Charles leaned back in his chair. "I would have sworn it was someone else who took a shot at me. Nonetheless, it's good to have closure on that concern."

Detective Gonzales said, "We still have the case of the Reverchon Park homicide to deal with."

"I saw the headlines this morning about another body being found there. Please don't tell me my business card was at the scene."

"No, Pierce," the detective said as he shook his head, "I guess you got lucky this time. If indeed it's Stapler who is committing these crimes, he might have exhausted his supply of your business cards."

"Stapler may be targeting a friend of mine."

"What do you mean?"

"I have a friend, Rachel Holbrook, who manages The Wine Therapist downtown. In fact, she's exhibiting some of my art there now."

"How did you get so lucky?" Gonzales smirked.

"She said a strange guy came in and inquired about one of my paintings. Rachel described him as creepy, almost homeless-looking. Like the kind of guy who would be more interested in how he was going to afford his next meal instead of purchasing art."

"And?"

"Yesterday, this guy came in right after Rachel arrived at the wine bar. Only the two of them were there. He asked her personal questions involving us, such as whether or not she was my girlfriend. One evening, I was driving her home from dinner and sensed we were being followed. It could have been Stapler. I'm really worried this guy knows where she lives. If he turns out to be Stapler, then I'm *terrified* of the possibilities."

"Is she working this afternoon?"

"Yes, she should be there."

"I'll stop by and talk with her."

"Would you like me to meet you there?"

"No, it's better if I do it alone. If this guy who's

harassing your friend is Stapler, it's about the only time he gets out of the uptown area."

"What do you mean, Detective?"

"He has been captured by the security video cameras at Reverchon Park several times both entering the park from the south entrance off the Katy Trail and the Maple Avenue entrance. Stapler has also been picked up by police security cameras on Maple near the Hotel Crescent Court."

"I know better than to tell you how to do your job, but couldn't you put some plainclothes officers in and around Reverchon Park?"

Detective Gonzales scowled. "Pierce, we just can't canvas the park every day hoping that we luck out with finding Stapler. That would take a lot of manpower which, quite frankly, we don't have at our disposal."

"I understand, but two bodies have been found in the park, perhaps the result of one perpetrator. That would seem like ample justification to assign whatever resources you do have to the area."

"I need to increase the probability that Stapler will be in a general area before I can assign those resources, as you characterize it."

"What about *me*? Can you use me as bait to lure Stapler say, for instance, into Reverchon Park?"

Detective Gonzales said in a tone fortified with sarcasm, "Are you going to text Stapler and ask him to meet you there?"

Charles smiled. "No, but Stapler knows where my

studio is located, and I'm reasonably certain he also knows where I live. What if I become very predictable in my habits?"

Detective Gonzales paused to let Charles's idea sink in. "It's possible that scheme may work." He sighed. "It's not customary, however, for police to use citizens as bait to nab criminals. In addition, it could put you in a lot of danger."

"I'm willing to assume all the risks."

"Are you on social media, Pierce?"

"Primarily just Facebook."

"That's perfect. If we do this plan, I want you to go on there and post the times you will be walking as well as pictures taken while you were outside. If we're lucky, maybe Stapler is following you on Facebook."

Charles raised his eyebrows. "I've never considered that as a possibility."

"Hold on a minute, Pierce, let me give some consideration to how I could set this up."

"That's fine. Please give me as much notice as you can so I can prepare."

"Will do."

"One last question, Detective. Is it all right if I let Rachel know you're coming by to talk with her?"

"That's fine. In fact, that's a good idea."

* * *

CHARLES HIT THE Speed Dial button to call Rachel.

"Hey, what's up?" she said.

"Hey, can you talk?"

"Yes, I can for a few minutes. Only one customer right now."

"It occurred to me late last night that the creepy guy may be the same one who threatened me in my studio. I talked with Detective Gonzales, and he wants to come visit with you about him. If I'm right, this guy's very dangerous."

"When does he want to talk to me?"

"This evening. I know it's a little awkward since you're at work, but he thought it was a good idea."

Rachel groaned. "This won't be good for business. Can't it wait?"

"I'm sorry. I'm sure he will be discreet. It's for your own protection, though."

"Okay, Charles. I need to go. Another customer just came in."

"Thanks, Rachel. Watch your back. Bye." She had already hung up.

At 7:30 p.m., Charles's phone rang. Detective Gonzales's name was on the screen. He picked it up. "Hello, Detective."

"Hello, Pierce. I wanted to let you know that I spoke with Ms. Holbrook a few minutes ago. I told her we would have a patrol car drive by her house several times each night for a few days."

"Thank you for that. How did she react?"

"The whole Stapler thing has got her spooked, but she appears pretty capable of taking care of herself.

She showed me a baseball bat she keeps behind the bar."

"I've heard her mention the bat before. However, I've never seen it."

Detective Gonzales laughed. "I suspect if you ever misbehaved, you'd get well acquainted with it."

"Have you given any more thought about me acting as bait?" Charles's tone turned lighter.

"Yes, I'll be in touch in a few days."

"Okay, thanks, Detective."

They hung up and Charles replayed their conversation in his mind, wondering how he could help them capture Stapler. Would he need a bullet-proof vest?

* * *

CHARLES WAS watching CNN at 11:00 p.m. and found himself falling asleep in front of the television. He turned it off and headed to bed, but was awakened from a deep sleep by his cell phone. After a few moments of struggling with the blanket, he managed to uncover himself enough to answer it. "Hello."

Rachel whispered, "Charles, he's tried to break into my house."

Shuddering, Charles shook himself to wake up and regain his senses. "Rachel?"

"Yes, did you hear what I said?"

"Someone tried to break into your house?"

"I just got home from work, and the doorjamb is

all messed up. I don't know if someone's inside."

"Call the police!"

"I just did."

"Good, now go lock yourself in your car, and wait until they get there. I'll get dressed and come right over."

When he arrived thirty minutes later, Charles heaved a sigh of relief to find two police cars parked in front of Rachel's house. He parked his FIAT Spider and jogged up to the front door. The door was cracked open, and the lights inside were on. He nudged the door open and yelled, "Rachel!"

She shouted back, "We're in the kitchen!"

As Charles approached, a police officer exited the kitchen and met him in the front hallway. Charles said, "I'm Charles Pierce. I'm friends with Rachel."

Another officer and Rachel then exited the kitchen. Rachel was pale and trembling. She said, "He wasn't able to get inside."

"Thank God," Charles said.

The police stayed another thirty minutes, posing various questions to both of them. Charles asked if they would notify Detective Gonzales and Charles's possible connection to the case. Before leaving, the officers walked the perimeter of the house, checking all the windows and the back door to determine if there had been any more tampering. One of them sat in his car in front of the house for an additional twenty minutes before driving away.

Charles and Rachel examined the damage to the

front door, trying to assess how to further secure it for the night. He said, "Would you like to come stay at my apartment?"

"No, I'll be fine. Thanks."

"But I don't believe it's safe for you to stay here until we get the door jamb fixed."

"I think I've got an old security door jammer in the garage. I can use that to secure the door."

Charles followed her to the garage. She rummaged through several boxes before finding the door jammer. "This should do the trick."

When they returned to the living room, she jammed one end snugly under the door handle, with the other end forced against the floor.

"It does seem to secure it," Charles said. "Let me go around and check it from the outside."

Charles exited the house through the back door, locked it behind him, and walked around to the front porch. He put his shoulder against the door and pushed. It did not budge. He went to the back door, and Rachel let him inside. "Thanks for coming over here," she said. "It probably wasn't necessary, but I appreciate it."

"Are you sure you feel safe enough to stay here?"

"Yes, I'll be asleep in five minutes."

"All right, Rachel, just call me if you need anything."

Rachel kissed Charles on the cheek and locked the door behind him. Charles strolled around the back of the house to where his car was parked. He surveyed the neighborhood for anything suspicious but did not see anything. The atmosphere was dark and still. Once behind the wheel, he circled around the block just to satisfy his own curiosity and then headed back to his apartment.

Gonzales better catch that guy right away, before he kills someone else.

CHAPTER 38

Two days later, Charles was walking in Klyde Warren Park when his phone rang. He pulled it out of his pocket. "Hello, Detective."

"Pierce, we're ready to proceed with stage one of our plan to bait Stapler."

"What is stage one?"

"We're going to target Reverchon Park specifically. I know you typically walk in the mornings, but for the duration of this operation, you're going to walk at dusk. How long does it take for you to walk from your apartment to the Katy Trail?"

"Maybe ten to fifteen minutes."

"All right, then I want you to begin precisely at 5:45 p.m. each day you walk. If Stapler is our guy, he'll feel more emboldened around twilight than he would in the morning."

Charles nodded.

"As we briefly discussed at headquarters, I want you to go on social media and document the times and places where you're going to walk. Be as specific as you can and post photos. Make it look like you walked in the park and took these photos every Tuesday and Thursday over a two-week period."

"I can do that."

"However, I want you to walk the same path just once. We don't want Stapler to strike until we're ready with the stakeout."

How smart is this Stapler guy, anyway? Will he figure out the photos?

"Also, be certain you're in range of the security camera at the south entrance of the park when you leave the trail for the park and again when you return to the trail after going underneath Maple. We'll be actively monitoring those cameras on the days and times you walk to keep a lookout for Stapler. After you've made these posts over a two-week period, give me a call. I'll then have you come down to headquarters for stage two. Is this clear?"

"Yes, Detective, I think I understand the plan."

"Good. Do you have questions?"

"Just one so far. Can you give me some idea as to what stage two entails?"

"Pierce, ever hear of a man-down transmitter?"

Charles sighed. "No. I'm not sure I like the sound of that."

"That's stage *two*. Don't worry, just give me a call when you're done with stage one."

"Okay, Detective."

Man-down? Better be Stapler and not me.

* * *

AT 5:30 P.M., CHARLES prepared to implement stage one. He put on his jogging sweats and runners and then sat monitoring the clock before heading out on foot toward the Katy Trail at 5:45 p.m. Rush-hour traffic had already kicked into high gear, giving him trouble crossing the streets. After almost twenty minutes, he reached the Katy Trail and another five minutes passed before he arrived at the south entrance of Reverchon Park.

As instructed by Detective Gonzales, he made certain to be in the range of the security camera as he walked down the steps to the park area. Charles had never visited the park at this time of day. A few people were milling about, but otherwise it was almost deserted.

By the time he was halfway to the Maple Avenue underpass, it was close to dark. The few lights scattered throughout the park presented an ominous visual. A slight breeze created dancing shadows on the grounds as it blew the branches of the century-old oak trees.

The sound of quick footsteps on the concrete path approaching from his rear gave him a sudden chill of anxiety. He spun around and stumbled, almost losing his balance. A jogger sprinted by and disappeared in front of him as he rounded a turn in the path.

Charles remembered he had not yet taken any photographs for social media. As he followed the path toward Maple Avenue, he snapped pictures every twenty yards. At 6:35 p.m., he spotted the Maple Avenue underpass. The only light on the trail was from a half moon and two streetlights positioned on the north and south sides of the street above. Charles debated whether to walk underneath Maple Avenue or to climb the stairs and cross the street above.

There's no way in the world I'm going to walk underneath Maple at night. Not tonight, anyway.

Charles snapped a few pictures of the path leading under Maple Avenue and dashed up the steps to street level. It was a whole different feel there, with noise and human activity that was absent below. He crossed Maple Avenue, exited the park, and hiked the slight incline up to the Katy Trail.

The trail was crowded with people. Some were doing their post-work jog while others were just enjoying fresh air. Charles headed south on the Katy Trail, stopping from time to time to snap pictures, then hurried home.

When he got back to his apartment, he sat down to catch his breath and placed two fingers over the pulse throbbing in his left wrist.

CHAPTER 39

Charles's phone rang at 7:30 p.m. "Hey, Rachel."

"I think he's inside my house."

"Stapler?"

"Yes, damn it! I just got home from grocery shopping. When I pulled up in the driveway, I noticed the light in my bedroom was on. I never leave that light on when I'm out."

"Don't get out of your car. Call the police, and drive down the street far enough away that you can still keep an eye on your house. I'll be right there."

Rachel sighed. "Okay. I'm getting sick and tired of this bastard!"

"You and me both. Now hang up and call the police!"

Charles rounded the corner onto Rachel's street and right away spotted her car. He pulled up alongside it. They both lowered their car windows.

He shouted, "Are the police here?"

"Not yet."

"*Damn!* Any sign of Stapler?"

"No, it's all been quiet."

A police car rounded the corner, accelerated past the FIAT Spider, and parked in front of Rachel's house. Two officers scrambled out of the squad card and hurried up to the front porch.

"Why don't you leave your car parked where it is," Charles said, "and come with me to your house?"

She nodded, locked her car, and jumped into the passenger side. Charles parked right behind the squad car. One officer stood on the front porch, and the other officer was out of sight. Charles and Rachel exited the Spider and made their way to the porch.

The officer said, "Did you call 911?"

"Yes, I live here," Rachel said. "I think someone broke in."

The other officer appeared from around the corner with a flashlight. "The bathroom window's been breached."

The officer on the porch said, "Ma'am, can you let us in the front door?"

Without a word, Rachel fished her keys out of her purse and unlocked the door.

The officer said, "Please stand back while we check things out."

Both officers crept inside the house with their pistols drawn. Charles and Rachel watched from the outside as different lights throughout the house were switched on.

Five minutes later, one of the officers appeared at the front door. "It's all clear. Come inside, and check to see if anything is missing."

Charles followed Rachel through the front door. She paused in the living room and spent a few moments scanning the room. "It looks like it did when I left it a couple of hours ago."

She followed this same procedure, going from room to room, making her way through the house. All the rooms examined so far seemed undisturbed. When she reached one of the bathrooms, broken glass was strewn across the tile where the intruder had smashed through the window.

Both officers waited in Rachel's bedroom. She and Charles entered.

One of the officers said, "I'm Officer Boyd and this is Officer Richardson."

Rachel nodded. "I'm Rachel Holbrook and this is Charles Pierce."

Officer Boyd pointed at the pillow on the left side of her bed. "Did you put this here?"

Rachel hurried over to her bed. Resting on the pillow was one of Charles's business cards. "Charles, come here. That bastard left one of your cards on my pillow."

The officers looked at each other, puzzled. Officer Richardson said, "This is your card?"

"Yes, Officer," Charles said with a long sigh. "This is the *modus operandi* of David Wayne Stapler. You can verify it with Detective Gonzales."

Officer Boyd said, "Can I see some ID?"

Charles pulled his wallet out of his pocket and handed his driver's license to the officer. Officer Boyd said, "I'll go check him out." He left the house.

Rachel reached down to remove the card from her pillow. Officer Richardson said, "Please don't touch that with your bare hands."

"It's my damn house," she barked. "I'll do what I please!" Rachel snatched the card off the pillow and studied both sides. "Something is scribbled on the back. What in the hell does 'TPC 22.011' mean?"

Rachel held the back of the card up so the officer and Charles could see it. Written by hand on the first line was *TPC 22.011*, followed with *See you soon!* on the second line.

"I've no idea what that means," Charles said. "Have any clue, Officer?"

"It looks like the perpetrator is either a criminal lawyer," Officer Richardson said, "or has spent some time in the prison library poring over law books."

Rachel said, "Why do say you that?"

The officer smirked. "Because TPC is the abbreviation for Texas Penal Code, and 22.011 is the code section that describes the elements of sexual assault."

Rachel punched her left palm with her right fist. "That pathetic piece of—"

"Calm down, Rachel," Charles said. "We're going to get this guy."

Officer Richardson had put on plastic gloves. "May I have the card, please?"

Rachel handed it to him. He slipped it in a plastic bag and made some notations on the bag's label.

Charles said, "How would someone like Stapler know the penal code section for sexual assault?"

"As I said earlier, prisoners spend their free time studying up on the law. Some of them go so far as to file their own appeals in court. There're a lot of jail-house lawyers. Also, it's possible this guy has been previously charged or convicted with sexual assault and remembered the code section for it."

Officer Boyd reappeared and handed Charles's license back to him. "Detective Gonzales verified your story. He's sending out a crime scene investigator to check for prints."

"Are you officers going to wait until the investigator gets here?" Charles said.

One of them said, "Yes, we'll wait in the squad car. You folks can wait inside, but don't go touching or messing with anything else until he's done."

The officers exited the house, and Charles and Rachel stayed put on the sofa in the living room. Half an hour later, a car pulled around the squad car and parked in front. A man in a suit visited with the officers a few minutes while he slipped on some protective gloves. He trotted up the sidewalk to the front door, carrying a small kit in one hand. When Rachel opened the door, the man introduced himself as Detective Ashford, Forensics, and indicated he would begin outside and then come inside.

The man left to conduct his investigation. After thirty minutes, he returned to the front door and announced he was finished.

"Did you find anything?" Rachel said.

"I took some prints. But most likely, they belong to you folks. I did find some blood on one of the shards of glass, so it's conceivable the perpetrator cut himself when he broke the window. We'll know more after the forensic exams."

After the investigator left, Rachel said, "I gotta go get my car. In all the excitement, I completely forgot about my groceries."

"Why don't you let me get your car? You lock the front door behind me. I'll pull into your garage."

"Okay, Charles, thanks."

When he eased her car into the garage, Rachel stood in the entrance of the door that led from the garage to the rear of the house, holding a hammer in one hand and a small rectangle of plywood in the other. "Once we finish bringing in my groceries, I'm going to take care of covering up my bathroom window."

"While you put the groceries away," Charles said, "I'll clean up the broken glass. Then we both can cover the window."

When they finished, it was almost 1:00 a.m. He said, "You're not planning on staying here tonight, are you?"

Rachel smiled. "Of course I'm staying here. Mr. Sex Offender's not going to scare me out of my own house."

"I had a feeling you were going to say that. Would you like me to stay and sleep on your couch?"

"No, I want you to go home and get some good sleep."

"Okay," he said with a grin, "you're the boss."

Rachel hugged and kissed him. "Thank you,

Charles, for everything."

"Not sure what value I added to the evening. Nonetheless, you're welcome."

On the way back to his condo, Charles checked his rear-view mirror every thirty seconds but never caught sight of a single vehicle behind him. *Where could that bastard have gone?*

CHAPTER 40

Every day for the next two weeks, Charles posted pictures on Facebook of his walking route to the Katy Trail and Reverchon Park. He was surprised at the number of people who either liked or commented on his various postings.

After two weeks, Charles notified Detective Gonzales that he was ready to proceed to stage two.

Detective Gonzales scheduled a 2:00 p.m. meeting at police headquarters on a Monday. Charles arrived at 1:45 p.m. and was directed to the same interrogation room where he had met with the detective on an earlier occasion.

At 2:10 p.m., Detective Gonzales entered the room and closed the door behind him. He carried a box, which he placed on the table as he sat down. "How are things with you, Pierce?"

"I'm doing okay, thanks."

"So you've been out there on social media posting your walking route and pictures, correct?"

"Yes, Detective, for two weeks, just like you instructed."

"Good." He popped open the lid of the box in front of him and removed a small, black device. He held it up for Charles to see. "This is a man-down transmitter. Do you know anything about these devices?"

"No, I'd never even heard of them before, until you mentioned it on the phone."

"Police use these transmitters as a surveillance body wire to listen to their inside man. If there's trouble, the operative can signal for immediate support using the duress call. That's this button." He pointed to a black panel at the opposite end of the device from the wire. "When it's activated, a silent alarm is generated, which will alert the rescue squad within a certain range. These devices also have another functionality, which is a fall-down feature. If the inside man is taken down, it will also alert the rescue squad whether or not the button is activated."

"That sounds handy," said Charles.

"In extreme situations, the rescue squad can use the tracking transmitter feature to determine the location of the inside man using a field-intensity directive receiver. The man-down device is sort of an electronic guardian angel. Does this all make sense?"

"Yes, Detective. I hope an extreme situation can be avoided, though, so a guardian angel won't become necessary."

"Pierce, are you sure you're up to this task? No one's making you do it."

Charles pursed his lips and nodded. "I'm sure."

Detective Gonzales turned the device over. "See this switch? This turns it on. The green light next to the switch indicates it's fully charged. You want to make sure that light comes on each time before you intend to use it."

"How long does the charge last?"

"It varies, but it should last for the duration of your walk through Reverchon and back to your apartment."

Charles said, "Let me hold it."

Detective Gonzales handed him the transmitter.

"It's really lightweight. Do I just carry it in my pocket?"

"It doesn't matter where you choose to carry it. Just make sure you can access it quickly if necessary." Detective Gonzales put the man-down device back in the box and slid it over to Charles. "Let's talk about how this is going to work. You'll have to be very punctual with following this routine."

Charles stared at the box without saying anything, until he couldn't focus on it any longer.

"Beginning next week, leave your apartment on foot on Tuesday and Thursday and take your usual path for getting to the Katy Trail. As soon as you exit your apartment building, engage the device. It could take a few minutes before the officers who are involved pick up the signal. Remember, when you enter Reverchon Park from the south entrance, stay in range of the security camera. As I said before, this camera and the camera north of Maple are being actively monitored on these days."

"What do I do if I see Stapler?"

"If Stapler approaches you or you see him, press the silent alarm button and stand still if possible.

If you don't encounter Stapler, keep the device on until you return safely to your apartment. Anywhere from three to five plainclothes police officers will be in and around that area of the park. They should be positioned so that at least one of them can get to you within a matter of a few minutes."

"That's comforting."

"There's one final thing. Try not to act suspicious. Be mindful of your body language. You're just a guy enjoying an evening walk through the park. Stop and take pictures and do whatever you would do under normal circumstances. Any questions?"

"If the police are in plainclothes, how will I know where they're located?"

"You won't. In fact, they won't be stationary. That area of the park is too large, so they'll have to keep moving. Any other questions?"

"I guess not, Detective."

"By the way, Pierce, I was sorry to hear about the break-in at Ms. Holbrook's house. We're continuing to send a patrol car by there from time to time."

"That's great. Thanks."

Detective Gonzales stood up. "Give me a call if you think of any other questions before next Tuesday."

As he drove home, questions flooded his mind. *How? Why? Where? When?* He had no answers.

CHAPTER 41

The next week on Tuesday at 5:00 p.m., Charles slipped on his sweatsuit and runners. His stomach churned at the thought of what the evening at Reverchon Park might bring.

The weather that afternoon was clear and in the upper forties. Charles exited his apartment at 5:40 p.m. and leaned against the exterior wall of the building until exactly 5:45 p.m. He switched on his man-down device, slipped it in the top pocket of his sweatsuit, and headed in the direction of the Katy Trail.

Never in his life could he have imagined a scenario where he would be wearing a police wire in a stake-out operation. His pulse raced as he weaved through the streets and parking lots on his path to the Katy Trail. He surveyed his surroundings, searching for anything out of the ordinary.

Charles reached the Katy Trail in eleven minutes without incident. The sun was fading into the horizon on his west as he walked north. He arrived at the south entrance to Reverchon Park and made certain he was visible to the security camera as he descended the steps into the park. While not crowded, more people were there than when Charles had last walked that path.

He tried to spot the undercover officers as he made his way north on his route. Charles encountered a man walking his dog and wondered if he was an officer with a trained police dog. Next, a jogger rounded the bend and stopped for a moment to tie his shoe, then jogged past Charles. The farther he walked on his route north, the fewer people he saw. A pair of women to his left sat on top of a picnic table, watching two toddlers play in front of them.

Charles decided to pause and snap some pictures of nothing in particular. He proceeded down the path and came within a few feet of Maple Avenue. He froze and stared at the entrance of the path underneath the Maple Avenue bridge.

The twilight evening was very soon approaching darkness. The streetlights on the north and south sides of Maple Avenue above were not lit yet. Maybe it was not quite dark enough for them to kick on.

Do I go underneath Maple or take the steps to street level?

Before he could decide, two joggers emerged from underneath the Maple Avenue bridge and passed Charles as they jogged south. He turned around and watched them as they faded into the darkness.

If joggers can do it, then damn it, I'm going underneath!

Charles entered underneath the bridge and hesitated a few seconds to let his eyes adjust to the low level of lighting. From past experience he knew he could not see the entrance from the other side until he was almost midway through the underpass. Due to the rain on Monday, the currents in Turtle Creek rushed louder than usual.

Charles took five more steps but stopped when to his left, some loose gravel slid down from the sloped concrete underside of the bridge. He walked again until something crashed right behind him. An adrenaline rush shot through his body. He reached for the man-down device to sound the alarm, but he fumbled it back into his pocket.

A man growled, "Hands out of your pockets."

Charles spun around to face the man, who swung a claw hammer at Charles. Charles turned and leaped away from the attacker. The hammer connected and pierced the skin on Charles's left shoulder blade. The impact and sharp pain caused him to lose his footing. He fell flat on the concrete path and braced for a second blow.

Another voice shouted, "Drop it, Stapler! You're surrounded!"

Charles froze, struggling to anticipate what would happen next.

The man dropped the hammer with a dull thud, and it clanged as it bounced on the pavement, coming to rest next to Charles's leg. Footsteps from all directions rushed toward them.

After a brief scuffle, the officers were able to overpower and apprehend the man. A voice familiar to Charles said, "He's cuffed. Get him out of here."

The voice belonged to Detective Gonzales. "You hurt bad, Pierce?"

Charles rolled over and sat up. He took several deep breaths. "No, he just winged my shoulder."

"Here, let me help you up." He pulled Charles to his feet.

Charles said, "I didn't think I activated the duress button."

"You didn't, Pierce."

"Then how did you know that I was in trouble?"

"Come on," Detective Gonzales said, "let's get out of this tunnel."

Both men walked to the north side and out onto the path. A police officer was in the process of putting a snarling David Wayne Stapler in the back of a squad car parked above on Maple Avenue.

"You didn't answer me, Detective," Charles said. "How did you know I was in trouble in there?"

"I had a hunch Stapler would make his play in this tunnel, so I hid inside and waited."

"Well, I'm certainly glad you acted on your hunch."

Detective Gonzales laughed. "Well, Pierce, I guess I must be your guardian angel." He clasped Charles on his unwounded shoulder and stuck out his hand.

"If that's true, Detective," Charles said with a laugh as he gripped the detective's hand, "I don't know if that's more unfortunate for you or me."

ABOUT THE AUTHOR

Jim Lively is currently the Artist and Curator at Martsolf Lively Contemporary in Richardson, Texas. After practicing law for many years, Jim decided to pursue his passion full time as a visual artist, film maker and author. He received the

2016 Merrimack Media Outstanding Writer Award for his second novel, *Punitive Damages. Surreal Absurdity* is a sequel to his third novel, *Aberrant Behavior.*His artwork and art films have been recognized in numerous juried competitions, publications, and film festivals. He has exhibited his artwork in several group and solo exhibitions across North America and Europe.

Fourteen of Jim's films have been selected to various film festivals around the world. His art film, *The Soul of Vinyl, Abbey Road Side 2.* screened at the 2016 New York City Independent Film Festival. Jim's film, *The Case of the Deranged Sommelier,* won Best Experimental Film in the 2016 Directors Circle of Shorts Film Festival and the 2017 Lion's Head Film Festival. His film, *Still Mad as Hell,* screened at the 2017 New York City Independent Film Festival. His latest film, *It's Gonna Disappear,* screened at the 2021 New York Flash Film Festival.

Jim's education includes a Bachelor of Arts from The University of Texas at Austin and a Juris Doctor from Southern Methodist University in Dallas.